EYES OF THE OWL

EYES OF THE OWL

Ante Miljak

Sterling House Publisher
Pittsburgh, PA

Sterling House Fiction
ISBN 1-156315-078-6

© Copyright 1998 Ante Miljak
All rights reserved
First Printing—1998

Request for information should be addressed to:

> Sterling House Publisher
> The Sterling Building
> 440 Friday Road
> Department T-101
> Pittsburgh, PA 15209

Cover design & Typesetting: Drawing Board Studios

All rights reserved. No part of this publication may be reproduced, stored in a retrieval system, or transmitted in any form or by any means—electronic, mechanical, photocopy, recording or any other, except for brief quotations in printed reviews—without prior permission of the publisher.

Printed in the United States of America

Every year millions of children are born, instilled with lethal values, and then turned loose upon a world which they destroy with frightening efficiency.

Only a revolutionary change of thinking will halt this tragedy.

"Eyes Of The Owl"
embodies such thinking.

This book is dedicated to my late father
Matè "Maćo" Miljak.

*Father, I did not always listen,
But I always remember.*

Acknowledgement

To my wife Lynn
Thank you...

1

The Air Botswana ATR-42 accelerated down the main runway of Johannesburg International Airport as Rurik watched the landing reflectors flash past the sombre profile of his twelve-year-old son Kito. As the aircraft rose, so did his hopes that the trip to the Okavango swamps would dispel from Kito's face at least some of the gloominess precipitated by Sandy's death three months ago.

In less than twenty four hours they would start the expedition Rurik had chosen for the challenge it presented. Even with an experienced guide, the journey through the primeval wilderness in the hollow tree trunk was uncertain. The dangers facing anyone who dared to enter the swamp in a flimsy mokoro, would make them focus their minds on the challenges of the present, and force them to forget the past and the future, he reasoned.

The eighty minute flight to Maun touched down at 10:20 a.m. Just over half an hour later their chartered Piper reached take-off speed and rose steeply into the shimmering haze of a cloudless African sky. It was not yet 11:00 when Craig, their scruffy-looking pilot, flicked a switch and the electrical current sped along the wires, retracting the undercarriage and reducing the drag.

The clang of the retracting undercarriage always made Rurik feel better. It made him believe the pilot was confident that they were safely on their way, and nothing in Craig's demeanor told him otherwise. Rurik didn't mind flying once the aircraft was on a cruising altitude, but the take-offs and landings made him nervous.

The swamp floated into view as Craig banked the aircraft and started turning north. A shimmering light reflected from the calm waters of the swamp's numerous lagoons. This was the place that, Rurik hoped, would restore peace into his and Kito's life.

Neither of them had yet recovered from Sandy's death, but Kito was devastated by the loss of his mother. Kito worried Rurik. In the three months since they had left the bay where the tragedy had occurred, Kito had changed from his healthy, dynamic and inquisitive nature, into a melancholic and lifeless boy. In spite of all Rurik's attempts to cheer Kito, he had not seen his son smile or show much interest in anything all this time. Desperate, Rurik searched for something that would help Kito and him fill the void left by Sandy's death and forget their misfortune.

When Rurik first mentioned the trip to the Okavango, Kito had responded with guarded enthusiasm. Their usual research about a place they were planning to visit had made them miss Sandy's presence even more. While in the past Kito and Rurik had studied wildlife and decided what adventures they would experience she had always been involved with the details.

As Craig levelled the airplane, a full view of the swamp revealed itself, stretching flat and wild to the curving horizon. On every side as far as the eye could reach, stretched a sea of fresh water, in many places concealed by a covering of reeds and rushes of every shade and hue. Numerous islands spread out over the surface and were adorned with rich vegetation, giving to the whole an indescribably beautiful appearance.

Rurik wished that Sandy was with them now, so that all three of them could experience the enchantment of the swamp, as they had experienced so many other incredible sights together. He pictured Sandy's big brown eyes looking at him, her smile expressing her happiness at them sharing another magic moment.

Craig stopped mumbling into the mouthpiece, closed the logbook he had on his knees and peeled off the earphones. He turned to Rurik and smiled.

"Well, now we can relax and enjoy the scenery for an hour or so. This bird has the sense of a homing pigeon. You can take off your seat belts. Is this your first trip to the Delta?"

"Yes it is, and we are quite thrilled about it," said Rurik. He looked over his shoulder at Kito whose green eyes were wide, observing the spectacle below. The rays of the morning sun made his hedgehog-like golden hair glow, but even the brilliance of the sunrays couldn't mask the sadness deep in his eyes.

"Kito, this is it! Another hour or so and we'll be at Seronga starting our adventure. Are you ready?" He knew his attempt to make his voice sound happy and carefree didn't fool Kito.

"Yes, I am ready. Are we going on the mokoro today?" He asked matter-of-factly but looked at Rurik with reproach.

"No, first thing in the morning. Today we meet our guide and accustom ourselves to the environment. By this time tomorrow we'll be deep in the swamp, facing the uncertainty of the uncharted African wilderness."

Rurik, mindful of Kito's silent rebuke, toned down his voice, but was determined to bring Kito out of the cocoon in which he had wrapped himself.

"Maybe Craig can tell us something exciting about the area." He added giving Craig a conspiratorial look.

"Have you been flying in this area long?" Rurik asked Craig.

"Two years in this area. Okavango, Chobe, Wanke, Victoria Falls. Another four years further north, mainly alongside the Rift Valley." Craig turned to Kito while he spoke, compelling him to join in the conversation.

Kito hesitated for a moment, as if considering whether or not to ignore this intrusion into his world. Seeming embarrassed by the attention, he finally asked, "How long is this valley?"

"It is almost as long as Africa. It stretches from the Red Sea in the north to the five thousand kilometer distant Kalahari desert in the south, which at two and a half million square kilometers is the largest sea of sand in the world. Cradled in the valley are the Nile river, Lake Victoria, Lake Tanganyika, Victoria Falls and of course the world's largest oasis, the Okavango, at its southernmost tip. Fifteen thousand square kilometers of swamp, known as the jewel of the Kalahari, lies in a great sea of three-hundred meters deep sand."

"Wow, that's some valley, it must be the biggest in the world." A spark lit up the dimness of Kito's eyes. He was fascinated by the magnitude of the valley. Inspired, Rurik prayed that this journey would draw his son out of despair and give Kito's life purpose again.

Mirth was more evident in Craig's pale-blue eyes than in his smile. "I don't know whether the Rift Valley is the biggest valley in the world, but I am sure it is the most beautiful." He stopped for a moment as if making a decision, and then continued, "Forces of such immensity that human imagination cannot comprehend them, have labored for thirty million years to create some of the most beautiful and mysterious sights on the planet. The Rift Valley is also evidence that these forces are tearing Africa apart."

"What do you mean by Africa being torn apart?"

Craig laughed, "Don't worry Kito," he said. "We are not going to slide into the ocean, especially now that we are in the air. I don't know the exact science of it but I know that measurements are being done regularly and each year the walls of the Valley are a few centimeters further apart. It has to do with the tectonic plates under Africa which are moving in divergent directions, but don't lose any sleep over it. It will take a few more million years before there is any danger of Africa splitting. By then we'll all be gone. Man will ensure that."

"What do you mean?" asked Kito. Pulled by Craig's magnetism he had moved to the middle of his seat and leaned against the front seats. Rurik glanced forward, checking the airplane was still flying level. It seemed that Craig was concentrating on talking and not on flying.

"Man has destroyed thousands of species and continues to destroy at least four an hour. By the time man realizes the consequences it will be too late to reverse the process which will lead to his own destruction.

I ran away from Europe, England to be more precise, because the only wildlife left there is people. I came to Africa, the continent where I thought wildlife still had a chance, but what I have seen over the past six years has made me change my mind. Soon all that will be left is a few game parks, until greed justifies the elimination of even those." Craig stopped suddenly, as if he didn't want to create any controversy. "Of course this is just my opinion. Some people don't agree with me," he added.

Rurik felt compassion for this man who criss-crossed the skies of Africa trying to run away from the encroaching realities of civilization. He wanted to somehow make Craig feel better and struggled for the words to express his sympathy. He knew though, that whatever he said would sound hollow because Craig was right. He too had run away once he had realized that man's current values, conceived by greed and ignorance led to unhappiness. Still, Rurik felt compelled to say something positive, "Well, the Okavango is still untouched, I believe," he said.

"Yes part of it is, but for how long? There is clamour to use the waters of the swamp more efficiently. Do you know what that means? It means using it for a diamond mine. It means using it for growing crops to sustain a population which breeds like rabbits. It means taking it away from an animal and the tree. The world has this noble notion that every man has a right to prosperity and freedom, and every ten or twenty years we have one billion more claiming this 'God-given' right. As has happened all over the world, sooner or later the politician in danger of being thrown out of office will sacrifice what he has to for his re-election. Here it will be the Okavango. And guess what, a balanced ecosystem will be unbalanced and all life below us will fall prey to the ultimate predator - man." Bitterness tinged Craig's words.

"Can't we stop this?" Kito asked, concern evident in his voice.

Craig, anger radiating from his eyes, shook his head angrily, "No." He said. "Forces driving this destruction are extremely powerful and are growing stronger by the day. The notion of human rights has become perverted and is sweeping the world like a flood, unchecked by human responsibility."

Craig stopped, aware that he had allowed his emotions to get the better of him, his drooping moustache stretched for what passed as a smile. Then he continued in a calmer voice.

"But don't worry Kito, you'll experience the swamp below in its virginity. It is still as pristine as it was when God created it. You must be careful of hippos, crocodiles and snakes, because they still rule down there. Do you know that the floods come in the dry season?"

"No, I didn't know. How come?"

"It is one of the many mysteries and paradoxes of the delta. In the rainy season the rain pours onto the mountains of Angola, a thousand kilometers away. From the eastern slopes of the central Angolan highlands the sister rivers Cubango and Culito start their journey in search of the sea. Although the Atlantic is only about three hundred kilometers away, they travel toward the three thousand kilometer distant Indian ocean and on this journey they join the Okavango river. Numerous tributaries add their waters to the now powerful river and six months later they reach the sea ... not the sea of water but the sea of sand. The rivers spread out in a fan shape for over a hundred kilometers in pursuit of the ocean, but the sand is endless. Their energy is dissipated over an immense area and the rivers abandon their unsuccessful quest and create a paradise on earth. We are above that paradise now." Craig paused.

"Wow," Kito exclaimed for a second time, his eyes wide open.

Rurik studied Craig as he spoke. Was all his talk about destruction, his emotional outbursts, his poetic portrayal of the delta designed to yank Kito out of his lethargy? Rurik looked into Craig's face but saw only the intense blue eyes and an untidy, week old beard.

"The journey doesn't end there," Craig continued. "Water travels deep into the earth, its destination still unknown to man."

Kito's head was now between Craig and Rurik. "Did anybody ever try to find out?" he asked.

Craig frowned, "Many have tried, but as far as I know, nobody has found out what happens to the water. But I am certain that someday, somebody will discover the secret. Man always does. Perhaps you'll be the one, but first you'll have to experience the swamp. A mokoro trip is a unique adventure."

Abruptly, the monotonous drone of the engine changed. Craig spun around and gripped the joystick with his left hand and the throttle with his right. The engine died. Gripping the joystick with his left hand, Craig pressed the starter button. There was no response. He pushed the starter a few more times but the engine remained dead.

"Craig, what's wrong?" Rurik demanded, fear choking his voice. Paying no attention to him, Craig grabbed the microphone, "Mayday! Mayday!" The urgency in his voice filled the cockpit and a gut-wrenching fear stirred in Rurik's stomach.

Clearly concerned, Craig looked at Rurik.

"Put your safety belts on," his voice was authoritative now.

Frantic, Rurik turned to Kito and saw fear in his son's eyes. "Kito sit behind Craig and put your safety belt on." Rurik could watch Kito there. Nervously he looked at Craig, "How much time do we have?"

"Not much. About two minutes."

Rurik glanced down at the swamp, vast and dangerous. An eternal stretch of reeds, water and treed islands came closer and closer. He spun back to his son. Questions flooded his mind. *Am I going to lose my son too? What have I done? I have lost my wife.* He wanted to scream *no God, not again.*

Bewildered, Kito looked at Rurik, searching.

What could he tell his son? What do you say to your twelve year old child, who barring a miracle, will die alongside you in less than two minutes?

Kito scrutinized his father's eyes.

Rurik knew Kito was looking for hope and direction, none of which was there. He would find helplessness and distress. Desperately Rurik searched for words. He searched in vain.

Kito's eyes widened in shock as he recognized Rurik's desperation.

Rurik couldn't hold his stare. In anguish he looked through the window, past Kito. Reeds, water and wooded islands, rushed at them. Time was running out. About a minute and a half Rurik estimated. What should he do? He was failing his son. He was failing himself. No, not now!

An unnatural calm descended on his mind. Rurik's eyes focussed on his son's and Kito's body tensed, ready for action. There was hope in the green eyes now. Rurik, now in control, spoke rapidly.

"When we are down on the ground or water, get out of the aircraft as fast as you can. If you are hurt, forget the pain, get out. Move away from the aircraft. That is very important. The aircraft might explode or sink. Don't panic. Think."

Craig banked the airplane to the left and Rurik saw an island with a clearing in the middle. They seemed too low to make it. Rurik focussed on Kito again.

"Think positively and use your common sense. Go the way the water flows. It will give you direction. South you have a better chance of meeting people. You know more than you realize. Think. Listen to your instinct. It'll help you make decisions."

Kito listened attentively to his words, and Rurik knew Kito's survival instincts were taking over.

"Dad, are we going to be all right?" Kito's voice shook.

"Kito I want you to be prepared for the worst. God will help us. Believe and be brave."

"Put your heads on your knees," Craig commanded, his voice tense and urgent.

Outside the window the top of the trees rushed by Kito's head.

"Kito, get down," Rurik shouted. As he bent down it struck him that he had forgotten the most important thing. Rurik whirled around and saw a blur of branches rushing past the window.

"I love you ..." was all he managed to say before the impact of the aircraft hitting the water sent him reeling forward.

The safety belt stopped his body, but his head shattered the window. Stunned, he felt a sharp pain in his spine. Flying glass followed the noise of the exploding windscreen and the aircraft came to an abrupt stop. Inertia swung Rurik's body back and pain shot through his left temple as his head hit the branch which had smashed through the windscreen. He collapsed, dazed. Warm, sticky blood ran into his left eye. The pain was blinding. Seconds passed. Everything was quiet ... too quiet. He tried to straighten but failed.

Rurik's blood dripped onto the rubber floor into a fast growing puddle. Then he saw a red stream creeping along the floor to join the puddle. Oh God! Was it Kito's? Dread squeezed his chest. Please God, don't let it be Kito's.

"Kito?"

"Dad!"

"Kito, are you all right?"

"Yes, are you?"

"Sort of."

"What's wrong?"

"I've been hurt."

"Is it bad?"

"I don't know."

Rurik groped for the joystick above his head and pulled himself up. Pain distorted his face as he straightened himself. His injured temple hit a branch and the sharp pain made him gasp. He moved his head away, leaned back into the seat and turned his head, his eyes just above the dead branch.

When he saw Craig Rurik froze. The other prong of the branch had impaled him through the chest. His face was stiffened in a grimace of pain, his eyes wide open. Blood poured down the branch.

Rurik shuddered. If the impact had not flung him forward, the other fork would have impaled him.

"Kito, get out."

"Dad, how badly are you hurt?" Kito's voice was shaking.

"I don't know. Get out and then you can help me."

"Dad, the door is next to you. I can't get out."

"Try to squeeze out next to my seat. If you can't, break the window. I'll try to open the door."

Rurik held onto the joystick with his left hand and with his right he pulled the handle, leaned against the door and almost fell out as it opened. He heard Kito gasp.

"Kito, what's wrong?"

"Craig is dead," he said in a shocked voice.

"I know. Get out. We are in the water. The plane might sink."

"Dad, where are you hurt?"

"My back. I can't move my legs. Get out. We must get away from the airplane."

Kito pushed the seat forward. Rurik gritted his teeth, the pain was excruciating. He held onto the branch and pulled himself forward and away from the door. Through the shattered windscreen he saw the slimy green water and a menacing semi-darkness. Tangled branches hung almost to the water and thick reeds grew along the edges of the swamp.

Kito squeezed past the seat and stepped onto the wing. The plane rocked. Rurik pushed the seat back and as his body straightened the pain in his back lessened.

Kito turned and the aircraft rocked again. The dead branch groaned. Rurik noticed that the top frame of the windscreen was resting on it. The wood groaned again as the plane tilted.

"Come on, Dad I'll help you."

"Take the equipment out first. Each item is absolutely essential for our survival. Knives, axe, pot, medical kit, rope, clothes, even the net has a value beyond imagination. Without it our chances are not good," said Rurik, knowing Kito wouldn't listen.

He didn't. He undid the safety belt, grabbed Rurik under the arms and tried to pull him out. Rurik was too heavy and Kito changed position. The aircraft rocked and the dead wood moaned, and then like a rifle crack the branch broke.

The front of the aircraft fell into the water with a splash. Kito lost his balance and had he not held onto Rurik he would have fallen off the wing. The aircraft tilted, as the other wing started sinking. Kito pulled again. His youthful arms gripped Rurik firmly and he succeeded.

Kito held Rurik upright, his body straining under Rurik's dead weight. Rurik began to slip. His legs dangled uselessly. He felt Kito's grip tighten. Seconds passed and neither of them moved. Pain tore Rurik's body and his soul.

"Kito, put me down and get our belongings," Rurik gasped. There was no response and he felt wetness on his cheek. Kito was crying. Rurik's eyes moistened but he fought back the tears. If he allowed emotion to take over now, they were doomed.

The aircraft tilted some more and the wing on which they stood slid down the sloping branch it was resting on. Then it stopped, balancing precariously.

"Put me down and get the equipment out of the cockpit. You must! For our survival," Rurik shouted, knowing they would die if they didn't act fast.

Kito stood firm, his body leaning backwards, supporting Rurik with his ribcage, his hands gripping his dad firmly.

Rurik tore himself away. Kito tried to hold him and failed, but succeeded in slowing the fall. Rurik fought to stay conscious.

"Kito get the equipment," he screamed.

Kito moved fast, causing the wing to slide down the branch. It stopped right at the edge, supported by a sapling. The branch was bent almost to the level of the water. One more movement and the wing would slide right into the water. Rurik looked at the cockpit.

"Kito, hurry up!"

Kito squeezed out of the plane, carrying their possessions in his hand and wiping his tears with the other. Rurik's heart went to his son.

"Kito, walk carefully. Don't rock the wing. We must get off this aircraft."

"We've got to get onto that tree," Kito said pointing to a tree that lay on its side, half of its roots torn out of the soil. Some of its branches supported it from the bottom of the swamp. Others grew upwards and sideways, giving the impression of a huge unfinished basket.

"Yes, go and put the equipment there. I'll pull myself along the wing. Then help me onto the branch. Just watch how you walk."

"Will you be all right, Dad? This plane is sinking."

"Yes. Go."

Kito walked, balancing on the wet wing. Ignoring the pain in his back Rurik pulled himself along the wing.

By the time Kito reached the end of the wing, it was pitching dangerously with both of them disturbing the precarious balance.

About a meter and a half away from Kito a thick branch arched from the water and joined the trunk.

"Jump," Rurik shouted.

Kito stood uncertainly. He looked back.

"Jump," Rurik shouted again, struggling along the wing. His forward movement disturbed the equilibrium and the wing slipped towards the water. Kito, forced to jump, flew through the air and landed on the branch. The wing rebounded, hit the water and began to sink.

Kito jammed the bundle into the fork on the branch and spun around, his body already in the air when Rurik shouted "No". Kito disappeared below the slime. A few long moments later his head broke the surface, a green cake resting on his head.

"Come on Dad, I'll help you."

Without hesitation Rurik slipped off the wing which was already under the water. He tried to swim but his legs were pulling him down.

Kito grabbed the neck of Rurik's shirt and towed him easily until they reached the branch. Kito climbed onto it and extended his hand to Rurik.

"No. Go to the trunk. I'll pull myself along the branch. You can help me out there. This position is dangerous. It's too close to the water. Take the equipment with you. Hurry."

"Okay, Dad."

Kito unjammed the bundle from the fork and crawled, slipping along the moist incline. Rurik scanned the water nearly missing the two periscope-like eyes watching him from the edge.

"Crocodile!" he screamed.

Frantically, he pulled himself along the arch, his body becoming heavier with each handhold, but fear gave him strength and he continued climbing. The branch seemed endless.

"Dad, where is it?" Kito shouted.

"On my right. At the edge of the water. Pull me out. Quickly!" Rurik felt Kito's hand grab his right wrist. He hung from the branch, his hips still in the water. Rurik looked for the crocodile again but saw only ripples on the water.

"Let go of the branch, I'll pull you up," he heard Kito shout.

As Rurik let go, his wet wrist began to slip through Kito's hands.

"Pull Kito! Pull!" he gasped, desperately trying to reach the branch again.

Kito pulled and Rurik's knees almost cleared the water, then they sunk back. His weight was too much for the boy.

"Hold tight," Rurik said. With all the energy left in him, he pulled himself up and grabbed the branch.

"Dad, hold onto both branches so I can move behind you and grab you under your armpits."

"Okay, hurry. I can't hold on for long." Kito moved behind Rurik and grabbed him under the arms and as Rurik pushed himself up Kito pulled him onto the branch. Rurik straddled the branch, his legs hanging down, his back against the trunk.

Kito stood on the two branches breathing hard, sweat running down his face, but his expression showed immense relief.

Rurik fought to stay conscious but black spots danced in front of his eyes. Kito's lean body moved out of focus.

"Dad, are you okay?" he heard Kito's worried voice coming from a distance.

"No, the pain is bad and I feel very weak," he managed to whisper.

"What are we going to do, Dad?"

Again, Rurik tried to focus and look into his son's eyes, but all he saw was a silhouette. He battled to stay conscious so he could give guidance to his son but he knew he had lost.

"Believe in yourself my son," he whispered using his last bit of energy and then he passed out.

2

"Dad! Dad! Wake up!" Kito sobbed. "Please Dad!"

There was no response. Kito grabbed his father's shoulders and shook him.

"Dad, wake up, please!"

Again there was no reaction. Kneeling, Kito hugged his father, tears clouding his vision. His boyish shoulders trembled with sobs.

"Please Dad, wake up!" He whispered repeatedly into his father's ear hoping he would hear and come back, but his father didn't respond.

Kito caressed his father's face and pleaded, "Please Dad, please. Don't leave me alone. I'm scared. I love you, Dad."

The blood had hardened into streaks on the left side of his father's face down to his chin and his bushy moustache curved around his upper lip like a caked, dark half moon. The left side of his face was swollen and an ugly, bowshaped sear ran from above his swollen eye to his cheekbone.

Kito gazed at his father's disfigured face not knowing what to do. He felt empty from crying and was so scared and lonely.

Kito looked around for the crocodile, aware his father's legs were hanging close to the water. He saw nothing but the slimy water and the sinking plane. The water was almost up to the windows and the slime was already closing over the sunken wings. He couldn't see Craig but the terrible wound on his chest was vivid in his mind. He looked at his father again. His short hair was almost dry. Kito decided to get some water and clean his father's face, hoping the water might revive him, but first he had to make sure his father did not fall off the branch. Kito stood up and gently moved his father's shoulders into the slight indentation in the trunk, so he would be secure while Kito brought a rope from the bundle. A groan startled him.

"Sorry Dad," he said, hoping his father was waking up, but there was no further response.

Kito climbed onto the trunk where he had thrown the bundle with their possessions, but the bundle was gone. It must have fallen into the water, he thought. What was he going to do? Tears filled his eyes again, as he walked along the sloping trunk and looked down, hoping to see the bundle in the water. He walked the length of the trunk and his heart jumped as he saw the net hanging from a protrusion on one of the branches. The net must have snagged onto the protrusion as it fell.

Kito ran up the trunk, lay down and extended his hand to reach the net, but it was too far. He inched closer to the edge and was just able to touch the nylon strand with the tips of his fingers.

He kneeled and looked around for something he could use to hook the net, saw nothing and was just about to lie down and try again when he heard a groan.

"Dad! Dad!," he called as he quickly climbed over the branches and jumped down to his father. His eyes were still closed and he looked the same as when Kito had left. Kito put his hands on his father's shoulders and shook him gently.

"Dad! Dad!! Dad!!!" The answer was a groan and slight movement of his head. Downhearted, Kito made sure that his father was leaning against the indentation and climbed back onto the trunk.

He had to get the bundle, it contained the first aid kit.

He lay right on the edge of the trunk, anchored the fingers of his left hand in a groove in the bark, pushed himself over the edge and hooked the net with two fingers. The nylon cut into his flesh as he lifted the bundle. The pain was more intense in the fingertips of his left hand and he knew he could not hold on for much longer.

As he pulled the bundle off the protrusion it swung against the trunk, its weight nearly pulling Kito into the water. The pain in both hands was equally intense now as he hung, unable to get up. With terror which grew proportionally to the numbness in his fingers, he wondered which hand was going to give in first. He either had to let the bundle go or he would fall with the bundle.

A groan shook Kito out of his confounded state. He jerked the net up, and when the bundle was at its apex, weightless for a fraction of a second, he shifted his upper body onto the trunk relieving the pressure on the numb fingertips of his left hand. Relief was short, and his scream pierced, for an instant, the unnerving melody of the swamp when he stopped the net's descent and a strand cut into his fingers.

Stable now, he pushed himself onto his knees. Kito struggled to untie the knots with his numb fingers, but felt more secure when he had on his belt with a large machete-like knife on his left hip, and the emergency kit in a leather pouch on his right. Kito grabbed his father's identical belt, knife and kit, a roll of rope, and hurried down to Rurik.

First he put the belt on his father, then unrolled the plastic rope, measured more-or-less, on the longer side, and cut it off. He spanned it across his father's chest and under his armpits, then tied it around the branch behind his head.

His father was secure now, but his legs were still hanging close to the water. He wondered whether a crocodile could bite through ankle high leather walking shoes with thick rubber soles, the best they could find. His father had always told him that in the bush shoes were the most important part of your clothing, because if you got a blister you became an invalid and a burden. With affection and respect Kito looked at his father's swollen and bloody face. He had to clean the blood off.

Kito tied a piece of rope to the pot and scooped up some water. Then he took his shirt off. It was splattered with his father's blood. Kito first rinsed it and then gently wiped off the blood, starting at the chin. For the most part the blood came off easily, however, his father's moustache and the indentation in his father's chin were difficult to clean but Kito persisted and his father looked much sturdier now with the lower part of his face clean. He was reluctant to start cleaning around the wound, and his father winced when he touched gently under the cheekbone, but he carried on as carefully as he could. If his father didn't recover, Kito knew they would both die. He felt tears well in his eyes and he wiped them away with the back of his hand. He thought of Craig and looked for the plane which was now totally submerged.

The rustle of reeds startled Kito and he turned to see a crocodile enter the water. Another followed. Both submerged immediately in the direction of the plane.

"Kito?" He nearly jumped at the barely audible whisper.

"Dad!" he shouted.

"You are awake. I was so worried Dad. I love you."

"I love you, too. Kito where are we? I have a terrible pain in my back. What happened?"

"Dad we crashed. Don't you remember? You are hurt. What are we going to do?"

His father's right eye was open, but it was misty and bloodshot. Seeming not to hear what Kito was saying, Rurik lifted his hand and wiped his eye as if to clear his vision.

Kito kneeled in front of him, his face strained. "What are we going to do?" he repeated anxiously.

As if his father had wiped the dizziness away with his hand the mistiness and redness cleared from his eye and he looked around the lagoon.

"Yes, I remember." His voice was stronger now. He focussed his eye on Kito. "We have to make a plan. Where is our gear?"

"On the trunk behind you. It's secure. I put your knife and the survival kit on your belt."

"Very good, there is no time for delay. In this position we cannot survive long. We have to make this place more secure." Rurik spoke quickly now.

"What do we have to do?" Kito asked with urgency.

"We must assess our position and our means very carefully. That'll help us use our resources optimally. From now on all we think is survival. Kito, you must forget every other consideration. Think survival only." Rurik's face was grim.

"What must we do first?" Kito saw how serious and worried his father was and realized he had been so concerned with his father's unconsciousness that he had forgotten about his back injury. Even though he was conscious his dad could not walk.

"We must find a safer and more comfortable place." Rurik said, and they both looked around. The elliptical lagoon, about sixty by one hundred meters long, was surrounded by trees, their branches hanging almost into the water. Only on the west side did an opening of papyrus and reeds allow the view of another wooded island.

Their surroundings seemed a perfect setting for a horror movie. Any moment, a monster could rise from the green slime.

Kito wondered how could they make their position safer and examined the tree on which they had found refuge. At the trunk the branches were thick. Two grew parallel to those on which they were sitting, and the third to the right of his father was about half a meter higher. All of them ran parallel for about four or five meters and disappeared under the slime in an almost perfect arch.

Kito watched as his father scanned the surroundings, his light eyebrows pulled together, his lips just touching under the bushy moustache. Then he looked down at his feet hanging less than a meter above the water. A patch of slime was stuck on his chest just between the two large pockets. He reached to take it away and a grimace of pain distorted his face, but then he took control. He peeled the slime off his shirt, flung it away and looked at Kito.

"First we must build a shelter and then find food. Then we look for a way out," he said.

"Dad, how are we going to do that? We have nothing!"

"We have some tools and we have brains. That'll do. Go bring the medical kit and make sure everything is secure."

Kito hung the pot onto the branch so it wouldn't roll into the water. Without the pot the bundle felt so light. He took out the small medical kit, carefully rolled the rest into a bundle and climbed down.

"Dad, here is the medical kit. What do you need?" Kito asked.

"There is an antibiotic spray in there. Spray some over the wound. It should prevent infection."

Kito shook the can, and as he sprayed the wound his father grimaced.

"Sorry Dad, but the wound looks deep. I had to make sure I sprayed enough."

"Okay, my son. We only need to spray again tomorrow and by then it should be much better. This is a very good antibiotic."

Kito took the medical kit and put it back into the bundle. He was distressed by the meagreness of their possessions.

"What's wrong Kito?" His father asked seeing his worried look.

"We have so little," Kito said.

"We have enough. Our minds are our best asset. Getting out of the swamp won't be easy, but we can do it. We must believe it. If we don't we are going to die. If we don't believe we can, we won't make it. You must believe we are going to survive. No situation is hopeless. Difficult yes, but never hopeless. We can make a problem big or we can make it small. It all depends on our way of thinking." His father took a deep breath and looked firmly at Kito.

"Imagine a chain of mountains beyond which you know is your home, the furthest peak barely visible. The mountains look foreboding and impassable. You are tired, but you have to get home.

The distance scares you. You doubt whether you can cross the mountains, but you have no choice. You have to get home. You struggle, but climb the first peak. From the top the second mountain is clearly visible and you realize that the chain consists of individual mountains. You climb one at a time."

The intensity of his father's eye captivated Kito. "What happens when you are on the first mountain and you are tired, but there are many more mountains to climb?" he asked.

"You'll be in the same situation as you were when you doubted the first time, but now you'll have one less mountain to cross and an invaluable insight."

"So what do we do now?" asked Kito.

"We make a platform here. That's our first mountain. Then we explore other options. This place seems more secure than camping on land. Take the axe from the bundle, but be careful with it. You'll have to chop some logs for the platform."

His father seemed certain and definite despite his injuries, Kito thought. He felt encouraged. The platform was a good idea, he wouldn't have to climb up and down all the time, he thought as he unfolded the net carefully.

The axe was state of the art. The blade and handle were forged from one piece of steel. Expensive, but unbreakable. He pushed the handle under his wide belt with the blade facing backwards and folded the net again. He made sure it was secure and was about to climb down when he saw his father's troubled face. He was looking toward the sunken plane.

Kito's sight blurred and he felt a tear drop. He mustn't cry. His father got upset every time he cried. His father always worried about him, especially since his mom had died. Kito had to be brave. It made his father happy when he was brave. He had to show his father that he was not a small boy anymore. Soon he would be a teenager. He would prove to his father that he understood the difference between being brave and being foolish. He had to show him *now*. Kito knew his father was distressed despite his courage, and he also knew that his display of bravery was mostly for his son's benefit.

"I have the axe," he said as he climbed down. He saw his father's eye was moist but pretended he had not noticed. Kito's heart went out to his father.

"You'll have to go onto the island and cut some palm trees. They are uniform, straight and long. Also they are abundant and the wood is soft and easy to chop. Don't lose the axe. Always hang it from your belt. It is your weapon and your tool. There are animals out there so be careful, but don't be scared. Remember the sharks we came across when diving or spearfishing. They went on their way without attacking. Usually it is the same with any wild animal. It will move away if it doesn't feel threatened." His father shifted his weight and grimaced with pain, but continued more strongly than before.

"Be careful and don't lose your way. Take markers and turn around to see them from the side from which you'll be returning. Use anything out of the ordinary as a marker. Cut logs to twice your height. We need about ten."

"Will you be safe here, Dad? Should we move you to a safer place? Maybe on the trunk?"

"That will take too much energy and time. We don't have time. It's nearly one o' clock. We have to have a platform by nightfall. I'll be all right. I only blacked out from exhaustion and pain. I feel better now."

"Okay I'm going. Shout if you need me."

"I will."

Kito embraced his father and kissed him on the cheek. He hugged Kito and held him firmly.

"Look after yourself, son." His father's voice shook.

"I will."

Kito walked down the angled trunk, axe in hand, intently watching the bush ahead. He squeezed between the roots and cautiously stepped into the knee-high grass. He scanned the area uncertainly.

This is the place of black mamba, swift and deadly. There is no chance of surviving a bite in the bush, Kito thought. Cold shivers went through his body as he pictured the evil head with two slits for nostrils which gave the snake an uncaring matter-of-fact look.

He had to go and cut the poles; his dad needed a safer place. At any time a crocodile could jump and bite his legs and maybe drag him down.

Holding his breath, Kito lifted his foot above the grass, carefully examining the ground before he took a step. He walked slowly, one step at a time. Something slid through the bush in front of him and he jumped backwards. He felt the blood drain from his face and his hands trembled as he examined the grass. He could see nothing. Kito stood still in the midday heat intensified by his fear while sweat poured from his face. After a few minutes he took a cautious step and another noise in the grass startled him. He wiped his forehead and gingerly stepped forward again.

Kito frequently heard movements in the grass and surrounding bush but he kept on walking. He saw birds and once a big lizard, as he headed toward the palm trees about fifty meters ahead. At the first strike of the axe the birds feeding on the trees scattered.

"Kito." The sound of his father's distant voice startled him.

"Yes Dad."

"Everything all right?"

"Yes. I've found the palms."

"Be careful, son."

"I will Dad."

Once Kito cut through the dry outer skin the chopping of the soft moist wood inside went fast. Soon he had two logs about three meters long.

While he was chopping Kito didn't immediately pay attention to a rustle in the bush behind him, but when he stopped to rest he heard the sound again. At first he saw nothing, but when he examined the bush more carefully he froze.

A hyaena stood about five meters away, her dull eyes staring at

Kito. Her drab, grayish-yellow coat, irregularly spotted with brown spots, camouflaged her well in the shade of the bush. Saliva was hanging from a jaw more powerful than a lion's.

Kito gripped the axe with both hands and faced the threat. The beating in his ears quickened with the rhythm of his heart. Motionless, he stood facing the hyaena. Kito's cotton khaki shirt was sticking to his back and he felt sweat dripping from his armpits.

He knew the hyaena was a scavenger but he had seen a documentary where a pack of hyaenas had defeated lionesses. Kito held the axe in his right hand and slowly backed to the end of the log, never taking his eyes off the animal. The hyaena did not move. He bent down and tried to lift one end of the log with his left hand, without success. He pushed the axe underneath his belt and then tried with both hands. The log lifted and Kito elevated it above his head. He bent, put his shoulder under the log and raised it, staggering under the weight.

Sweat was biting at his eyes, but he couldn't wipe it away with both his hands balancing the log. If the hyaena attacked he would throw the log at her, he thought. He had to pass within a few meters of the animal to get back to his father. Motionless, the animal watched him struggle. Kito stepped towards the hyaena. The scavenger took a step backward and then stopped as if deciding whether to attack. For a few seconds it stood still, and then it turned and walked on.

Relieved, Kito staggered under the weight but managed to carry the log. Finally, he placed it on the trunk, slowly straightened and stretched his aching body. The front of his shirt was wet and his face itched. He wiped off bits of grass and bark that had stuck to his wet hair and face.

"Dad, I'm back and I have a log," he called. For a moment there was no answer. Kito was about to call again when he heard his father clear his throat as if something had lodged there, and then he heard his muted voice.

"Well done my son. You are a big boy and I am proud of you."

Kito felt deep love for his father. He knew how he suffered at being disabled. Kito was sure that if his father had not been injured he would have found a way out of their predicament. He always said to Kito that a problem is a challenge, and that a challenge makes a man.

Kito heard him clear his throat again, before he continued in a strong voice.

"I heard chopping, the tree falling down, the sound of chopping again and then there was no noise. I got worried and was going to call when I heard you putting the log onto the trunk. Was it hard?" he asked.

"It wasn't so hard. It wouldn't be bad if it wasn't so hot." Kito rested the log at the top of the trunk now and he could see his father's face. His eye was red and swollen.

"It is very hot, but it took you only half an hour for one log. At the same rate it will take you another four and a half hours for another nine logs. You'll be finished before dark."

"Dad I have chopped two logs. I just have to bring the other one."

"Kito that's great. Rest then for a while, before you go back. It'll get cooler. You must preserve your energy. There is enough time," he said gently.

Suddenly movement in the approximate position of the aircraft caught Kito's attention. The monstrous head of a crocodile had surfaced. The slitted, drooping eyes fixed on his father and then the reptile submerged. The only sign that the crocodile had been there was a few small ripples.

"Dad. Crocodile!"

His father looked in the direction of Kito's pointed finger.

"Where?" he asked alarmed.

"It went under again."

"Bring that log down, so we can put it under my legs." Rurik's voice rose.

Kito grabbed the log, as his father tried to lift his legs with his hands. Only the rope across his chest prevented him from falling into the water. He looked down, his shoulders tense as if expecting a blow.

"Dad can you take the end of the log and I'll slide it down?"

"I can, but be careful you don't throw me off balance. Rest the log on the branch on which I'm sitting and I will hold it until you come down."

Glancing at the water nervously, Kito manoeuvred the log next to his father's head and slid it down, while he guided it onto the branch.

"Hold it. I'm coming." Kito jumped down and they guided the log into position across the parallel branches, anxiously scanning the water. Once the log was in position, Kito cut two pieces of rope and tied it onto the branches. His father groaned in pain as Kito lifted his legs one at a time and put them over the log.

"Sorry Dad, but now you are safe."

"Kito, I can't stay in this position for long. The pain is killing me. Bring another log so I can sit on it. My legs are too high. There is to much pressure on my spine. Hurry!" his father gasped, his face distorted.

Kito jumped and ran down the trunk and into the bush without stopping, oblivious to any rustling or movement in the grass or bushes. He staggered under the weight of the log as he ran back. Within minutes he pushed the log under his father's legs. The log now in a convenient position, Kito lifted his father and with his foot he pushed the log underneath him.

"Thank you Kito. This is much better," he said breathing a sigh of relief as he looked at Kito with respect.

The pride and admiration in his father's face suddenly changed everything. Kito felt as if he had grown up in an instant. He wasn't a child anymore and could take care of them. He looked to the west across the papyrus, his trepidation evaporating in the face of his growing confidence.

"Dad, now that you are safe, I'm going to cut some more logs," Kito said, his breathing back to normal.

"Kito, rest a little bit before you go; there is enough time."

"I'm fine Dad. I'm going."

"Okay. I'll try to catch us some fish while you are gone. See if you can find some worms or insects under the dead bark." His father's voice was almost joyful now that his legs were not hanging close to the water, and Kito's spirits rose.

His father opened the pouch on his hip, pulled out a metal container and put it on the log between his legs. He made sure the container was stable before he rummaged through it and as he lifted a sheet of malaria tablets he exposed a pile of banknotes. He took out the money and smiled.

"This is my emergency supply," he said waving the notes. "Remember my son, the value of this paper is always debatable. It is worth nothing now. Only our abilities are of any value. On the other hand perhaps this paper has some value - we could use it to start a fire," he chuckled.

Kito caught a grasshopper, a large moth and a few beetles and left his father fishing while he went to cut more logs. Every time Kito brought a log his father complained about the fish having eaten the bait. It seemed that the pain had eased and he was in better spirits.

Kito positioned the logs apart to make the area bigger and filled the gaps with papyrus stalks and reeds. By late afternoon a three by two meter platform was finished. His father was sitting comfortably, still complaining about the fish.

When Kito was satisfied that the platform was as good as he could make it he erected the tent and then sat down and watched his father fish. He hadn't been sitting for more than five minutes when there was a pull on the line. His father tried to hold the fishing line but it slid through his fingers.

"Kito, help me!" he shouted excitedly.

Kito jumped to the edge of the platform and caught the fishing line. Even though it fought hard, between them they managed to pull the fish towards the platform. Finally, it was out of the water wriggling in the air. One more pull and it would be on the platform.

As Kito bent down to catch the fishing line for the final pull, the water erupted. Open jaws zoomed towards his face and he watched the distance between the jaws and his head diminish. He couldn't move. He couldn't even scream. Then, for an instant the picture froze and then the jaws snapped closed. The crocodile splashed back into the water with the fish in its jaws, the fishing line trailing behind. Still immobile with fright Kito watched the place where the crocodile had disappeared and started shaking uncontrollably.

"Kito! Are you all right?" he heard his father shout but he could only stare into the water.

"Kito!" His father shouted again, louder. Kito slowly turned to look at his father, feeling as though he was going to faint.

"Are you okay, son?"

"Yes Dad, but scared out of my wits." Kito's legs were shaking as he walked over to his father. He sat down and leaned his head on his father's shoulder. His father's arm shook as he embraced Kito's trembling body.

"At least we know there are fish in this lagoon," his father said in an attempt to sound cheerful.

Kito pressed his head hard into his father's shoulder and they sat in silence, staring ahead.

After a while Kito felt his father's arm squeeze his shoulder. "We have to try and catch another fish. Give me the fishing line from your kit and we'll tie it to a branch so we don't lose it again," he said.

"Dad, what if the crocodile snaps the fishing line and takes the fish again?"

"We have to keep on trying. We need food. It is unlikely the crocodile will get the fish again. We can also bend the branch and tie it down with a quick-release knot, so once the fish is hooked, we can release the branch and it'll bring the fish up fast. Remember the mountains. We must keep trying."

Kito stood up, bent a thin branch and tied it with a quick-release knot to the log. He put the fishing line over the branch and lowered the hook into the water. At the same time his father tied the other end on the log next to the quick-release knot. When the fish took the bait, all they had to do was release the knot and the branch would shoot upwards, flinging the fish out of the water.

"The crocodile won't beat this contraption," his father said with vengeance.

Kito smiled. "I'm going to make a hook for the pot and then get some mud for the fireplace," he said

"Now that's positive thinking - making a hook for the pot before there is something to cook. Bring some firewood as well, before it gets dark," his father said jokingly.

"You always tell me that positive thinking brings positive results. I hope you are thinking positively and it will bring you a fish." Kito quipped.

"I'll catch the fish and you just make sure that you bring enough wood." Kito heard his father's voice behind him.

First Kito brought mud on a palm leaf and made a circle on the platform and then an armful of wood and a half meter long green branch. He cut the offshoots with a knife about five centimeters away from the central branch and made a hook for the pot which he tied on a branch above the circle.

"Where is the fish? Everything else is ready," Kito said turning to his father.

"Make a fire, then everything will be ready."

When the fire was burning Kito leaned against the trunk "Now everything is ready, where is the fish? Are you still thinking positively?"

"I am. We have shelter, we are functional and have the necessary tools. There is plenty of water and we have a good chance of catching a fish."

"Even with a positive way of thinking how do you know that we will succeed?"

"I don't, but one thing I know for sure, we have to keep trying. We must not be discouraged by our failures but learn from them. Out of every experience, good or bad, there is a lesson to be learned. A positive approach is the only and right way. If you fell, would you lie on the ground in fear that you might fall again if you got up? That would mean if you fail once you have failed forever. I can assure you, with that kind of approach you wouldn't find one successful person in the world. All the world would be lying down, too afraid to stand up.

In our present situation we would think that we are lost, I am injured, and the swamp is a dangerous and endless place. We would think we had no chance of getting out. If we had thought like that we would still be hanging on the branch and by tomorrow we would more than likely be dead, unless by some incredible coincidence somebody found us."

The sudden rustling of leaves in the still, early evening cut the conversation short. The branch was being jerked down by the fishline. Quickly Kito's father released the knot and the branch shot upwards, the fish flew in an arc as if flung by a catapult out of the water. Its tail was flicking as if it were still swimming through the water. When it hit the platform it jumped wildly, ungracefully. Kito pinned the fish down, took out his knife and cut off its head.

"Well done Kito. The crocodile isn't going to get this one."

"Nope," Kito said with satisfaction.

"There is enough food here for today and tomorrow. Tonight we grill the fish on the spit and tomorrow we can make soup from the head. Put the head into the pot so the flies cannot soil it," Kito's father said, excitement radiating from his eye.

"Dad, you clean the fish and I'll make a spit." Now that they had food Kito was much more confident about their survival. His father was right; they had to keep trying.

The first star had appeared in the western sky by the time they had the fish turning above the fire. Across the fire Kito watched his father deep in thought, turn the fish. He was probably planning what to do tomorrow; he always thought about tomorrow. What'll happen tomorrow? Today had been a hard day but they had a platform and food. When his father had asked him that morning to make a platform, Kito didn't think he could do it. His father looked so vulnerable and totally dependant on him and that drove Kito against fear. His father didn't look so vulnerable now, his face was thoughtful but calm. He didn't seem to be in so much pain and the swelling on his face seemed to be lessening.

Their situation had changed dramatically since the crash and it was difficult to believe that they had accomplished as much as they did. From a hopeless position their positive attitude and love had brought them through a trying day.

Kito remembered the water erupting and the crocodile flying towards his face and shivered. His father looked at him.

"What's wrong Kito?"

"Nothing Dad, I was just wondering if crocodiles are good to eat?"

"Yes, especially the tail. Why?"

"Why don't we catch one?"

"Catch one!? How?"

"Remember when the crocodile took the fish?"

"Yes."

"It jumped out of the water to get the fish. If we hang the fishhead as bait maybe it'll jump out to get it, then we can catch it in the net." As Kito talked a picture was forming in his head.

"Kito, that's brilliant. We wouldn't have to worry about food for weeks. Tell me more, I am sure you have a plan," his father said enthusiastically.

"Yes I do. We should bend a strong branch and tie it down on one end of the rope. We then hang the net tied by the four corners from the branch. On the other end of the rope we hang the fishhead as a trigger to release the branch. If the crocodile jumps and takes the head the knot will be released, the branch will shoot upwards and bring the net up with the crocodile in it."

"Brilliant my son, your idea is truly brilliant. You have such a clear mind. Let's work out the mechanics. We have to decide which branch to use, how to bend it and how far down it should be tied."

"I think we should bend it as far down as we can and position the net about half a meter under the surface so when the crocodile jumps up for the head, he will be above the net." Kito couldn't contain his excitement.

"What if the net comes up to the level of the platform and the crocodile gets onto the platform. We would be in grave danger."

"Dad, not so long ago you kept telling me to be positive. Are you negative now?"

"No my son, I am just cautious. In your planning you must always take into account the negative aspects of the situation, so you can be prepared for them."

"We prepare ourselves. We make some weapons to fight the crocodile if it lands on the platform."

"Kito, you are right. We can make some spears to keep the net away and if necessary we can fight the crocodile. It looks like the fish is ready. Let's eat."

Kito ate with appetite, but he saw that his father had difficulty in chewing and swallowing. His left eye was still closed and badly bruised.

"Dad, are you in pain?" he asked.

"Yes. My back is sore, especially when I move. My head feels better now, but my temple hurts when I chew. I think tomorrow you can massage my back. Perhaps my spine is only stunned and hopefully I'll regain the use of my legs when the swelling is gone. The cut on my temple doesn't worry me too much, but we must just spray it occasionally to prevent infection."

"I'll spray it after supper."

"No Kito. We spray tomorrow. We must look after this spray, it's all we've got.

The fire had died down by the time they had finished eating, and in the absence of any wind to blow the ashes the coals were greying at the edges. Their world contracted with the diminishing intensity of the flame. Kito looked at the stars in the west, reassured that the other world was still out there beyond the light of the fire. The smell of the swamp was less musty in the relative coolness of the evening.

His mom had always told him that each person had his own star. When that person dies, the star dies. He wondered where his star was, and how long it was going to shine.

3

"Dad, you look much better this morning. How did you sleep?"

"Not very well. The pain in my back kept waking me and I had nightmares. Maybe you should massage my back a little; it might help," said Rurik, immediately regretting not being more positive. "But, I feel much better," he added.

Kito kneeled beside Rurik and pulled his shirt up, exposing his back. "There is a big swelling on your back, just above the belt," he said. When he touched the swelling Rurik stiffened from the pain and gritted his teeth as Kito's inexperienced fingers massaged the swelling.

"That's enough," he gasped after a few minutes.

Kito tucked Rurik's shirt into his pants and stood up. "What are we going to do now?" he asked.

"Make a fire. Then we eat."

"Why a fire? It's hot already." Kito questioned.

"We must keep a fire burning in case of a search. You'll also have to find two saplings for the spears which we have to harden over the fire," Rurik said. Analyzing their plan during the night he realized how dangerous it was for them to try and catch the crocodile. There were so many uncertainties, yet the advantage was enormous. For weeks they would be able to concentrate only on getting out of the swamp instead of trying to catch food, a task for which they were ill-equipped. The uncertainty and impending danger depressed Rurik but he didn't express his doubts to Kito. Kito had to believe he would win.

Kito didn't seem to have a confidence problem. After breakfast he cut two saplings about three meters long and about three centimeters in diameter. Rurik sharpened them and paying special attention to the tips, hardened them on the fire.

Kito tied the rope to an above branch with a quick release knot. They bent the branch as much as their strength and ingenuity allowed and tied it to the branch next to Rurik. Kito cut the other end of the rope so it hung about half a meter above the water. He would hang the fishhead at the end and when the crocodile pulled on it, the quick-release knot would untie and the branch would shoot upwards.

Kito measured and cut four equally long pieces of rope, tied them to the short rope on one side and to the four corners of the net on the other. He hung the contraption from the branch.

The net rested on the slime, and with the spear Kito pushed it under the surface. The four ropes resembled a pyramid with a green base, a rope hanging from its apex to just above the water. Satisfied that the trap was ready, Kito tied the fishhead on the end of the hanging rope.

Rurik watched as Kito worked efficiently and with purpose. He thought it ironic that the main purpose of their trip had been achieved.

"It's ready," Kito said and turned to Rurik.

"It looks good. If the crocodile takes the head the branch should bring him above the platform, but dependant on weight it might bring him on a level with the platform or even below it. If the net stops on a level with the platform the crocodile could slip onto the platform. If that happens try to push it off. Watch for both the tail and the jaws. They are equally dangerous. If you cannot push it off the platform jump onto the trunk."

"What about you?"

"I'll fight too, but you mustn't get hurt. Kito, this is *very* important. With both of us hurt we won't stand a chance.

If something should happen to me you can make it on your own. Make bundles out of papyrus and tie them together. That's how the natives make rafts. They have lived here for hundreds of years, with less equipment then we have now. Go south. In the morning the sun has to be on your left. You know how to orientate yourself. The natives learned by observing nature; so can you. Watch the monkeys. You can eat anything they eat. Always think before you do anything. Plan everything. Kito, promise me that you will do as I ask."

"I'll do as you say, but I will fight for you and I will not leave you," Kito said defiantly.

"Kito you must not get hurt. You have to survive."

"We'll both survive," Kito said with confidence and turned to survey the swamp. He resembled an ancient hunter as he squatted at the edge of the platform with the spear in his arms. There was no sight of the crocodile. In silence they waited.

The flies, attracted by the stink of the rotting fishhead buzzed irritatingly around their heads and landed on their sweating faces in increasing numbers. The combination of the sun and the fire made the oppressive midday heat unbearable. Kito stood up and stretched his legs.

Eventually the reeds parted and the crocodile's head appeared. Kito hit the rope with the spear and the fishhead jumped, causing a swarm of flies to temporarily abandon the head and then settle back on it. Kito squatted on the platform, his body alert.

The crocodile ignored the provocation; its monstrous features watchful. Kito swung the fishhead again. The crocodile slid into the water and submerged without creating a ripple. Seconds passed and the surface of the water remained undisturbed.

Kito was too young to fight a reptile, Rurik thought. Then the water erupted and like a missile the crocodile shot towards the target. Open jaws closed around the fishhead and the crocodile continued to travel the downward curve of his trajectory, pulling on the rope and releasing the knot.

The branch shot upwards and the net flew out of the water intercepting the crocodile's path. The momentum of the upward movement swung the net away from the platform distancing them from the image of ferocity; blunt teeth attacking the net and a furiously lashing tail. The net swung back. Four scaly legs protruded through the opening, frantically trying to get a hold as the crocodile flew towards Kito.

Gripping the spear, Kito jumped back and before he could react, the net swung away. Kito waited for the net to swing back and then he lunged, stabbing at the crocodile with the spear. The only effect the blow had was to push the animal away and drive it berserk. Then the first four millimeter thick nylon strand broke. Kito waited for the net to swing back and stabbed again, and again the net just swayed away. A few more strands broke.

Tormented by the reality that his distance from the battle was too great to make a difference, Rurik watched the showdown impotently. If the crocodile broke free over the platform they were in trouble.

"Get him Kito! Take a proper stance. Kokutsu-Dachi!" He screamed, his voice hoarse.

Kito's stance changed. His weight moved onto his back leg, the knee slightly bent, his front leg barely touching the platform. As the net approached he thrust the spear at the reptile's underbelly. As the tip of the spear touched the skin, Kito's back leg straightened and his weight shifted forward driving the spear through the skin, just below the neck. The frantic animal savagely attacked the net tearing it as easily as a spider's web. Blood ran down the spear onto Kito's hands and fell onto the platform, making it red and slippery.

"You are a star, Kito! Do it again! As he loses blood he'll grow weaker." Petrified Rurik tried to give Kito encouragement.

Kito's blood smeared hands thrust the spear again. It penetrated the skin and disappeared into the belly of the animal. The crocodile twisted its body, recoiling from the repeated blows and tearing the net into tatters. Each time the tail moved with less vigor and the spear took longer to penetrate the skin. The boy had won.

With slow deliberation Kito turned and looked at Rurik, his red hands holding a bloody spear. His face was shining with sweat, pride and splashes of blood. Then he started shaking.

Rurik tried to talk but triumph and pride stopped the sound in his throat. He stretched his hands towards his son. "Come," was all he managed to say.

The boy walked to his father and Rurik embraced him. Gradually, Kito stopped shaking and regained his composure. He stood up and swept his hand theatrically in the direction of the crocodile. "There is a skin for your shoes," he said.

"It's just like you to give me a half finished product. When are you going to learn?" Rurik teased.

"You're never satisfied," Kito complained. The words stung Rurik. He was proud of Kito, but the briskness of Kito's voice told him that he didn't think so. Rurik had always encouraged Kito to do more, to push his limits, not because he was not pleased with his performance, but because Rurik believed that the child needed encouragement. He did not want Kito hindered by the perceived limitations of a degenerating society.

He was aware that the last few months they had not communicated well. Rurik had not been happy with Kito's state of mind after Sandy's death. His own efforts to occupy himself with his business had forced him to leave Kito alone, exacerbating his bitterness and feelings of alienation. More than ever Rurik appreciated how privileged he was to have a son like Kito.

"I *am* satisfied now, my son. You have given me something of unsurpassed value. You have given me hope. I am proud of you and I always have been. You have to forgive your dad for an occasional slip."

Kito's shoulders straightened and he smiled happily. He turned to look at the crocodile. Its tail hung limply over the side of the net as blood dripped from its wounds.

"We must get the crocodile onto the platform," Kito said.

"Okay, hold the rope until I untie it. Then pull the net and I'll slacken the rope. Be careful that the net doesn't pull you into the water if the rope slips through my hands." Rurik was apprehensive again.

Kito pulled on the rope which Rurik was untying with one hand, at the same time helping Kito pull with the other. When Rurik loosened the knot the rope slid over the branch. Rurik grabbed it with both hands and stopped the slide. He then slackened the rope while Kito pulled the net onto the platform. Finally the crocodile lay stretched from one end of the platform to the other.

Kito hacked through the scales on top of the tail and through the vertebrae, cutting the tail off. He untied the two corners of the net. They pulled on the rope again and the torso rolled off the platform splashing water all over them. Three crocodiles leaped from the reeds and dived into the water. After a few seconds the torso abruptly broke the surface, its light underbelly facing up. Kito and Rurik watched the feeding frenzy, as the three predators fought over the dead body in a melee of turning bodies and lashing tails.

As the body tore, one by one the crocodiles dived to bury their bounty in the mud where it would rot to tenderness. Fascinated by the raw violence and somewhat subdued by the awareness of their vulnerability, Rurik and Kito silently proceeded to preserve the meat. Kito cut the tail into strips while Rurik made a smoking platform.

It was only three months ago, Rurik thought while he weaved a grid, that he had been an athletic and healthy forty-year-old, capable of any feat. He had a great son and a radiant wife who both loved him. The intensity of his love for them was unequalled by any other emotion. Love, he had found, was the crucial ingredient of happiness.

Now he was crippled physically and weakened emotionally. Without Kito he would be helpless. Luckily, Kito's interaction with nature had prepared him to deal with life-threatening situations and had taught him to be observant. Diving in places that sharks frequented had taught Kito that contrary to the disinformation that caused millions of sharks to be slaughtered, there was magnificence in the creature portrayed as a mindless killer. He had learned to assess his odds.

Riding the breakers behind Black Rock had given Kito an understanding of the ocean currents. He learned that the current took you out to sea but it also brought you back to shore. Rurik remembered watching him pass the tip of the foreboding rock, gliding down on the slope of a wave while white foam boiled behind him. He remembered the feeling of pride the picture had evoked in him then. Now that same feeling grew in his chest as he watched Kito confidently slicing off the few remaining strips of meat. Kito pushed the skeleton of the tail over the edge, but the splash didn't provoke a response.

"Dad I don't think all this meat will fit on the grid you've made. I'll hang some on the branches above the fire. This meat should last us for weeks," Kito said looking for a convenient place to hang the meat.

"I am sure it will. Put some meat aside for us to roast, it's been a busy day."

By the time they had started to roast the meat, the song of the swamp changed unnoticeably into its night tune. Kito bit off a piece of meat and chewed cautiously at first. "This meat tastes like a mixture of lobster and chicken," he said with surprise as he ate hungrily.

The taste of the meat pleasantly surprised Rurik. "I am sure it is as nourishing. The meat on the lower smoking platform is already hardening on the surface. As soon as the surface is hard we should hang it up and then put the meat from the branch onto the grid, so that it won't spoil."

"What are we going to do tomorrow?" Kito asked as he put some more wood on the fire. The moist wood smoked for a while and then flames leaped and pushed the darkness away.

Rurik thought for a moment then said, "We have to move on. Now that we don't have to worry about food we can plan our departure. We'll start by building a raft first thing in the morning. You'll have to cut papyrus and I'll tie it into bundles. Once we have enough bundles we'll tie them together to construct the base, then we can position a row of bundles along the edge for added comfort and security. The raft should be big enough to be stable, but not too cumbersome to push through the reeds and channels. We'll also have to make two paddles and a pole for shallow waters."

Kito's reaction was apprehensive, "Dad, I am a little scared to go into the swamp after seeing the crocodiles fight today. This place is full of crocodiles."

Rurik wished he could avoid sending his son into danger but he knew that it was the only way they would survive. He cleared his throat to make sure his voice was strong.

"Kito I know you are scared. It is natural to be scared in an unfamiliar environment. There is even danger on this tree. Some of the most poisonous snakes in the world like the black mamba and cobra, live in this area and some might live on this tree. If we don't see them doesn't mean they are not there. We are not free from danger anywhere in the swamp. Our survival depends on taking risks because we are facing an immense challenge. We get out or we die. There is no other option. You'll have to overcome your fear and go and cut papyrus. That is a risk you have to take. I have no doubt that we'll face many dangers and that you'll have to make some hard decisions. You might have to save yourself if you cannot save both of us. If both of us cannot survive, you must survive."

Rurik stopped talking because he knew the lump in his throat would make his voice tremble and he didn't want Kito to notice his weakness.

"Dad, you keep telling me that I must leave you in case of an emergency. I would never leave you. Please don't ask me again to leave you," Kito pleaded in an apprehensive voice.

"Kito, I keep repeating myself because you don't want to accept that a situation might arise where any attempt on your part to save me could result in both of us dying. That would achieve nothing. You must think rationally and you must do as I say. If you have to - leave me!" Rurik felt as though his chest was going to burst, but fought not to show his feelings.

"No Dad, never! We'll make it together." Kito was on the verge of tears.

"Kito, don't allow your emotions to make you act illogically. The situation we are talking about might never arise, but if it does you must be prepared. There are times in your life when sentimentality has to be suppressed in order to make rational decisions." Rurik knew he couldn't control his emotions for much longer.

"Dad, you are wasting your time. I will never leave you." Kito was stubborn.

Rurik felt tears moistening his eyes, but he managed to hold them back and in his struggle he forced his left eye open. Sternly he looked at Kito. He hoped Kito would detect the hardness he wanted to project. Rurik had to persuade Kito that his approach was correct, knowing full well that he himself wouldn't act in the manner he advocated. He tried to think of an argument which would break Kito's determination and remembered a heartbreaking story that had been ingrained in his memory ever since he had read it as a teenager. Rurik looked at Kito sitting expectantly on the other side of the fire and decided to hurt his son.

"I'll tell you a story about a father and son which I read when I was about your age." Rurik kept his voice deep so it wouldn't quiver. "It might help you to understand the logic of my words."

"I'll never abandon you." Kito's voice was definite.

"I'll tell you the story anyhow. It happened in the time of early industrialization. The father was a chimney sweeper and he cleaned tall factory chimneys. It was a dangerous job, dangerous but good. It fed the family, gave him his self-respect and made him his own man. Those were the days when adults and children worked in semi-slavery in factories. Being a free man was, and still is, worth more than money."

In the fading light Rurik watched his son's disinterested face and hated himself for the pain he was about to inflict on his boy.

"In those days the son would normally continue in the father's trade. The boy in question was sixteen years old and for some time the father had been teaching him his dangerous trade. He impressed upon his son that safety was all important and any mistake could be fatal." Rurik could see Kito's interest rising.

"Remember when I taught you to climb trees? To support yourself on three points? Two hands and a leg, or two legs and a hand."

"Yes I remember."

"Well, that was what this father taught his son and he repeated it frequently. He told him under no circumstances to act otherwise. The boy was annoyed with his father's repetition, as you are with mine now, but he listened because his father was very strict about his education and the boy also knew that if he slipped off the chimney he would not survive. But one day he made a fatal error. He wanted to show his father how brave he was and make him proud. They were on the top of a tall chimney and he walked on the edge towards his father, without holding. He tripped and lost his balance."

The light of the fire played on Kito's intense face as he stared, riveted, at his father.

"The boy tried to catch onto his father but the father moved away and the boy fell to his death."

Kito gaped at Rurik and waited for the condemnation of the father, but Rurik kept quiet. It took a few seconds before Kito realized that no condemnation was forthcoming and his reaction was violent, but predictable.

"How could the father do that? He didn't love his son!" he said with bitterness.

"He loved his son very much, more than himself," Rurik said, sadness in his voice.

"Your logic stinks. I cannot believe you are saying this. The father was a coward. He should have been hanged." Kito spoke with disgust.

"That is what everybody said at the time," Rurik's voice was calm but an emotional storm raged in his soul.

"What do *you* say?" Kito spat the words out.

Rurik faced Kito across the dying fire. He couldn't see Kito's eyes clearly, but he could sense his anger.

"It doesn't matter what I say. What matters is what that father thought at the time. He was standing on the narrow wall of the chimney lowering the brush down and leaning against the rail, both of his hands busy. The father saw his son fall and try to grab onto him. He knew that if that happened they would both die. The boy was the oldest. If both of them died the family would lose their breadwinners and slide into poverty." The expression on Kito's face was one of confusion and Rurik continued.

"Both the father's choices led to hell. Sometimes life is cruel and forces upon us cruel choices."

Kito lowered his eyes and looked into the fire, his shoulders drooping. Sadness and disappointment were in his voice when he asked, "What happened to the man?"

Sorrow was in Rurik's voice when he answered. "A few months later he died from a broken heart, condemned by society. Nobody but his family came to the funeral."

"But why. Couldn't people see he was suffering?" Kito asked, downhearted.

"Society didn't want to acknowledge his pain but found pleasure in inflicting it. Misplaced self-righteousness is a prevalent trait in society. Condemning somebody else makes people feel superior."

For a long time they sat in silence looking into the last few burning coals. Rurik's feelings were in turmoil. He knew he was hurting his son, and love fought reason. Love told him not to inflict irreparable damage to his son's security; reason insisted that he had to. Rurik searched for a compromise. Kito didn't. His shoulders straightened and the silhouette of his head against the western sky was stark, as were, Rurik knew, his green eyes.

"What would *you* have done?" The tone of Kito's voice discounted any compromise. He was insisting on an unambiguous answer.

Rurik continued looking at the cinders, wiping away the mist from his eyes. He would gladly give his life in exchange for Kito's.

He was all Rurik had left and without him there would be no happiness and no future.

"I would have done what I had to do." Rurik's soul wept.

"But what *would you* have done?" Kito wanted a commitment.

"That I cannot tell you. I was not in the position of that man."

"Dad, if it was me in the place of the father, I would have tried to save you."

"But you could have fallen to your death, too. What about the rest of the family?"

"I don't have the rest of a family. I only have you." His voice quivered.

The screams in Rurik's soul drowned the sounds of the swamp. With hands around his knees, Kito leaned backwards, and then a sniff broke the silence.

"Please my son, don't cry." Rurik wished he could walk to his son and hug him.

"You don't love me." A sob came with the words.

The deafening screams in Rurik's soul shattered reason and he moved forward, but a sharp pain in his back stopped him.

"Kito you cannot say that. You know I love you." Rurik fought to control his voice.

"No you don't. Mom loved me, but you don't. I miss mom. I wish she was here." Hurt and bitterness forced the words out.

"Kito, you know that is impossible. I miss your mother as much as you do, but now there are only the two of us. My son, you know I love you."

Kito's sobs were the only reply. Rurik listened to his boy's sobs and wanted desperately to hug him, to comfort him, but he knew he had to let him cry. Kito would feel better once the tears had taken away the hurt and disappointment.

"Kito, put some wood on the fire." Rurik said after a prolonged silence, anxious to divert Kito's thoughts with some action.

The wood obstructed even the little light shed by the amber coals and now Rurik could hardly see Kito's silhouette through the smoke which brought tears to their eyes. A while later a small flame flickered from the dried bark and then the flames erupted lighting the faces of the two lonely people who were confused by their feelings and the direction their lives had taken.

As if he had been awakened, Kito looked at Rurik and in a subdued voice asked, "Dad, tell me about Mom."

"What do you want me to tell you?"

"Tell me about the first time you met."

Rurik's thoughts travelled back to the remote bay where his dreams had been realized and then shattered. An image of white sand and desert-like dunes stretching to a small rocky bay on the left, the imposing black rock on the right and a little stream, almost hidden by white sand, unobtrusively flowing into the ocean, was imprinted in his mind. A hint of the reef beyond the breakers for those who knew, a mystery of the deep for those who didn't, brought exciting memories to Rurik.

Rurik remembered gazing at the curving horizon, his burdens diffusing into the tranquillity of undisturbed nature.

"Dad, what are you thinking?"

"I was just remembering the day I met your mother. It was a confused time in my life. I had come to understand that material wealth did not necessarily bring happiness and I had also realized that walls of deception surround individuals. I longed to let go of my walls and reveal myself to myself. I had come to the bay in the hope of finding a way in which I could reconcile my life with the true values by which I knew I should live. I'd begun to recognize that I would have to choose between the values of society and what I believed were true values. I was searching for the strength and conviction to help me face the challenge." Rurik's eyes shone with zeal as he spoke.

"I watched the waves being born and within minutes, dying, to become part of a new wave. I wondered about the purpose of the wave and the purpose of my life. I couldn't find an answer to either," he continued, a faraway look in his eyes.

"This day I was sitting on the dune when I saw movement in the direction of the rocky bay and decided to sit and wait to see who else had braved the almost impassable roads in this part of East Africa. The movement of arms became progressively visible, hypnotizing in their repetition. I was mesmerized and sat there gaping. The last thing I had expected to see in this desolate place was the girl of my dreams."

Rurik looked at Kito who was listening dreamily and he was sure Kito's mind was also back in the bay, his birthplace.

"The first thing I remember about your mother is her bright smile, her red, yellow and blue flowered bikini. She had come to the bay to study a small black lizard that only lived on Madagascar and at Black Rock. She was preparing for her masters degree in marine biology and had just arrived to live at the conservation station. Well, you know that abandoned house. She was still familiarizing herself with the area.

The sudden appearance of a beautiful girl in the bay startled and excited me. It was love at first sight. You see, from the beginning I was impressed by your mom's clarity of thought and her practical nature. Her laugh was as crisp and clear as a mountain stream. Her hazel eyes were deep and bright and for the first time in months I was happy.

This was my woman I thought. The girl of my dreams, feminine and innocent. We spent the afternoon walking on the beach and talking and with each minute I was deeper in love and I hoped she was too. My problem was that I was planning to leave the following morning and on the way to the bay of rocks I told her so.

She seemed disappointed and that made my heart jump. She cared I thought. I had a project on the go and the deadline was in four weeks. She thought that that was a lot of time and asked what kind of project it was.

I explained to her about the advertising agency I owned and how hard I fought for the contract and that there was not so much time as there was a lot of work to be done. Then I told her that the project was an ad campaign for electric toothbrushes.

She looked at me and then burst out laughing and said that she was sure mankind could survive without those. I was hurt at her laughing about my job and I showed it in my voice when I told her that not every job is as important as studying lizards was, but as unimportant as my job was I intended doing it well. She apologized and said that she couldn't associate me with advertising electric toothbrushes.

I was annoyed because I knew she was right. I did the job for money and not for the fulfillment. For the first time I realized why my life was going in the wrong direction and why I wasn't happy. I was not doing a worthwhile job. It was ridiculous. I had to go back to persuade people to buy something they didn't need, and leave this beautiful bay and beautiful girl.

The sun was hanging above the horizon as we reached the top of the dune and the red glow from the western sky tinted crimson the foam of the breakers.

I was just about to tell her that I wanted to see her again when she asked me to stay another day or two. She said that if I worked a little harder I would be able to catch up.

I looked at the black rock and saw the foam on the top of a big wave rolling toward its destruction. As it smashed into the rock the wave created its own song, a song of spray in the red sunlight, high above the black rock. It was like a thorn bird that sings the most beautiful song while impaling itself on a thorn, to die.

I will stay, I said.

She threw her hands around my neck and kissed me. I held her warm, slender, sun-tanned body, and knew my life had changed. Reluctantly she wriggled out of my arms, turned around and ran down the slope. I watched her run, my future suddenly more certain. She stopped just before the path curved, turned and waved at me, and then the bushes hid her figure as the sun sunk beyond the horizon. I was lonely again."

Kito engrossed in the romance, waited for Rurik to continue, but realizing Rurik had stopped he looked at him and asked, "What happened the next day and when did you decide to go and live there?"

"I'll tell you more some other time. Now we have to go to sleep, because in the morning we must start making the raft before it gets too hot. It will be safer to cut papyrus while it is cooler. Crocodiles are not as active in the cool mornings. Now pour some water onto the fire in case the wind comes up. The tent could catch fire."

"Okay Dad, but promise you'll tell me more."

"I promise."

Kito helped Rurik into the tent and Rurik heard the hissing of the coals as Kito poured water over the fire and darkness closed in. Feeling his way Kito then crawled into the tent. The closing zipper was the last unnatural sound in the night of the Okavango.

4

Like a snake winding its way between the reeds, the mokoro glided on the surface of the swamp hardly disturbing the still waters.

The old man pushed the pole into the mud with a precision born of experience, propelling and directing the craft at the same time. His eyes were focused on the swamp ahead, choosing his way. The reflection of the blue sky in the clear water made Madala feel as if he were travelling between two worlds. Tall reeds grew towards both worlds, a sky above and one below, joining at the level of the water. He guided his craft in-between cone-shaped clusters of spearlike leaves which slanted high above his head.

Madala listened to the whispering of individual leaves sliding alongside the dark wood of the mokoro and pondered on his reflection travelling through the silent world below. He wondered if he was one or two people. Since he had fled from witnessing the annihilation of his world, the discord within him had deepened and his reflection had changed. His face had become lined and his eyes had grown empty.

For over twenty years now he had been called Madala—the old

man. Then, it was a name of respect, but now he would be called the old man because he *was* old. He knew that if he were able to watch his reflection now, he would see an old man, stiff of body, straining to push the pole against the bottom of the swamp. The strength was draining from his body daily. His movement was more restricted now than seven years ago when he had shaped this mokoro out of the great Makutshumo tree. African ebony, as the white man called it, lasted the longest.

It had taken him a month to shape a prow into the centuries old, living trunk. When he was hungry he had climbed the tree to eat the delicious fruit that grew on the branches which reached thirty meters into the sky.

For two months he had dug out the wood with a selepe. Many times he had to sharpen the hoe-shaped axe, wearing away the sharpening stone, as the hard wood had worn away his selepe. It took another month to trim the outside with the curved petwana he had inherited from his father. He had combined all his experience and his knowledge of the swamp to shape a craft which he knew was the last he would have the strength to make.

The unblemished trunk had given him a mokoro, unrivalled by any he had seen before, a fitting monument to the great tree. As he had trimmed and shaped the wood it had changed color from pristine white to pink and then to red, as if feeling the pain from his curved adze.

When finished, the angled prow resembled a striking cobra as the mokoro lay on the ground covered by thousands of wood chips. Uniform and three fingers thick, the sides curved slightly towards the rear where the flat bottom ended in a semicircle. He pushed the mokoro into the water, and for five days he had kept it submerged, so that the wood wouldn't crack. During that time he made a pole from the silver leafed Mogonono tree and rested for the journey.

Over the years Madala had driven his boat into secret places in the swamp, places where only a man with his experience and knowledge could go. The young generation kept to the tourist route along well-established channels. He was one of the last people who could utter with confidence the saying that was the heritage of his people: "We are like a current of a mighty river that cannot be stopped. We make our way through the thickest thicket." This did not apply to the new generation.

In Madala's youth, every member of the BaNoka tribe had intoned the saying with pride, but their self-esteem died with the arrival of the hunter, mine recruiting official and finally, the adventurous tourist. Masters of the swamp had traded their freedom for the prosperous world of money, and now dug gold from deep underground in the city far south, his people called Egoli, the city of gold.

Once a year they had come back and told stories about the wondrous city of Johannesburg and its fabulous wealth. They had brought with them things which made them different from the people of the swamp, things which only money could buy. They also brought jealousy. This changed the tradition where the most successful hunter would stop hunting for a while, waiting for other hunters to equal his performance and receive their share of adulation.

Driven by jealousy and greed, the young followed the trail to the city, and as the years passed fewer and fewer returned. Those that did come back brought exciting tales and unknown diseases; more left and more died. New values negated the old and the BaNoka faced extinction. Disease killed Madala's wife and his children left to look for a better life.

Madala, alone now, except for his reflection, guided his mokoro through the reeds that became thicker the further he went. Now he was travelling along a tunnel, the space narrowing with every push of the pole. He wondered if he shouldn't have chosen another route, but he had never been this way before, and there was always the hope that in an unexplored place he could find peace and the Spirit of the swamp.

This wasn't the first time that his mind had examined the reflection gliding through the silent world below. The loneliness which had deepened through the years of a solitary existence made him desperate for companionship.

This morning the image of his reflection was vivid and Madala felt sorry for the thin old man straining to push his craft through the serene world of water. He pushed the pole harder, forcing his way through the reeds. Why had his life turned out the way it had?

He focussed on the image hoping he might get some hint of the reason, but the man below was as inscrutable as ever when Madala tried to fathom the enigma of life. The vein on the left side of his forehead which stretched from above his left eye and disappeared into the grey curly hair on his temple seemed more prominent today; as were the two deep grooves which stretched downward from just above each flattened nostril and ended in a curve below his lower lip. Scattered white hairs above his upper lip joined two tufts of sparse gray beard on his chin and framed an island of a few curled white hairs below his lower lip. His deep-set eyes, shaded by a high brow and circled by hundreds of tiny wrinkles, were focussed on two puddles of water spreading on the floor of the mokoro.

Madala knew that as soon as he was out of the reeds he would have to bail out water. Although most mokoros ooze from the time they are made, his mokoro never had. But time, sun and water had affected the hardwood and after years the water had found a weak spot.

First he had to get out of the reeds, he thought. It required all his willpower to force the mokoro through the thicket. Doubt invaded his mind and for the first time in his life he feared he might get trapped. The fear stimulated his mind to extract the maximum energy from his feeble muscles and by the time he saw the first water lily, a sign that the reeds would become sparser, his strength had almost deserted him. With the last of his energy he broke out of the dense reeds and drove above the wide leaves of the waterlily whose red, brown and pale green stems leaned in the direction of the water flow. Suddenly the reeds stopped and a lagoon opened in front of the exhausted old man. On the opposite bank the Mopani forest was reflected in the placid waters, the tips of the tallest trees lit by the rising sun still hidden behind the forest.

Madala stopped poling and kneeled to bail out the water with a Coca-Cola tin. Every time he used the tin it reminded him of the civilization from which he had escaped and of the guilt with which he had lived.

He had returned to the still untouched swamp, where no beer and Coca-Cola cans rusted between the stalks of the papyrus. He kept the can though, because it was the best container for bailing water. He could never forget the massacre anyhow. He had attempted to justify his actions by claiming a lack of understanding because of his youth. He was only thirty five then, but he realized that no justification could reverse his deed.

He wished now that the hunter had never come to his reed village and that he had never taken him to the places of the crocodiles. When the hunter came, Madala had been a respected man in his village despite his youth. He was a cunning hunter and the best mokoro maker. The white man was hunting crocodiles for their skin. He had heard that Madala had tested his mokoros through the "thickest thicket", so he asked Madala if he would help him hunt the crocodiles, seeing that he knew the swamp best. In payment he would give Madala a rifle and many bullets. In addition, the hunter would give his people money if they helped him skin the reptiles.

When Madala had seen how easy it was to kill with a rifle, he agreed. In the future he would be able to kill without effort, instead of having to endlessly stalk the animal to bring food to his people.

The BaNoka chopped the trees to make more mokoros and then drove them into the swamp in search of the crocodiles. They killed mercilessly and everybody grew richer. As more hunters came to hunt fewer crocodiles there was competition for the best trackers. Wages increased and the hunter paid Madala per skin. Hyaenas and vultures followed the killers closely and gorged on the carcasses that littered the swamp, their bodies swollen from excessive food;

even for the scavengers there was too much. They had hunted for five years and killed thousands of crocodiles. Madala was rich.

Then a black mamba struck. Madala's hunter died in terrible pain, half of his body swollen and black. Madala and his people sold the skins to other hunters and returned to their village. His mokoro leaked badly and now that he wasn't hunting he had time to make a new one. The first Makutshumo he had earmarked years ago wasn't there, neither was the second. He came across many signs of mokoro making before he found a tree. He realized that soon there would be no more trees and no more mokoros. Nobody could live a hundred years waiting for a young tree to grow, and when a hundred years passed the knowledge of mokoro making would be gone, and the BaNoka too. Without a mokoro, the man of the swamp was dead. It dawned on Madala that what he had done was unforgivable. He also understood that when all the crocodiles were gone the crocodile hunter would become extinct too. By destroying the crocodile, the crocodile hunter destroyed himself and by cutting down the trees the BaNoka cut their roots. Madala wished then that he could undo what he had done and longed for the way life had been, before the hunter had come. But time and his deed stood between him and that life.

Depression overwhelmed Madala and with nostalgia he thought about the times when he had tested his mokoros and explored the swamp. He had felt he belonged there and every new place he discovered had made him feel richer. He had hunted and prayed for the spirit of his quarry to go in peace and enter the great Spirit of the swamp. He would return to his people content in the knowledge that his spirit was in harmony with the Great Spirit that combined the spirits of all people, animals and trees, dead and alive.

After a long search for a suitable tree, Madala had shaped his mokoro, his spirit overwhelmed by the realization that his world would disappear if the destruction continued at the same rate. Madala knew he had to do something to stop the destruction but felt powerless. Maybe the white man who had initiated the destruction had the power to stop it, Madala thought. He returned to the village, and inquired with any white man passing through, about a person who could help him. Many laughed at him, but eventually he met a missionary who told him about a man called Doctor Adams who fought for the rights of animals.

For two days Madala drove his mokoro and on the second afternoon he reached Dr.Adam's camp. He was a short, scruffy looking individual, barely taller than Madala. In an offhand manner he listened to Madala's story and his desire to stop the destruction of his world. Dr.Adams looked unimpressed and almost bored as he sat on a canvas folding chair and listened to Madala who squatted in front of Dr.Adams and wondered if he had not wasted his time. However, this was the best occasion he had had to tell his story and he had decided to at least finish, now that he had come so far. The pain he felt was evident in his voice. What gave him some reassurance was the fire in the intense blue eyes when Madala's emotions caused his voice to rise. When Madala finished his story, Dr.Adams stood up, restlessly walked around and told Madala that he couldn't help him.

He had no power to stop the killing, he said. All he did was gather information about the disastrous effect which the spread of civilization had on the wildlife. He had managed to attend a few conferences and present his findings, but nothing had really changed. He had continued to fight because there was no worthier cause to which he could dedicate his life. He had been accused of insensitivity to the needs of people who required space and resources, but he would continue to fight and Madala was welcome to join in if he was prepared to take care of his own needs.

Madala stayed and over the years he and Dr.Adams became friends. Dr.Adams taught him how to read and write and gave him books on various subjects. Madala learned about the philosophy by which the civilized world lived, and realized it was in conflict with all other life.

For twenty-seven years he stayed with Dr.Adams and they recorded the destructive activity of man. They recorded that cattle and fire killed certain grasses and allowed others to spread unhindered. The new growth was favorable to wildebeest and they became so numerous that they destroyed their own food source and starved. They recorded grasslands turning into deserts, as cattle grazed permanently, on grasses that were able to sustain only a migratory population.

They recorded the story of the hunter who said that he wore out thirteen barrels on his rifle shooting crocs, and the saying that the two most lethal animals in Africa were the cow and the veterinary surgeon.

They recorded hundreds of thousands of animals dying against the three hundred kilometers long Kuke fence, which had been erected on their migratory route and prevented them from reaching the waters in the north. The destruction was massive and swift. Devastated by the impact of "civilization", Madala couldn't bear to record anymore.

When Dr. Adams went to yet another conference to present their findings, Madala told him of his decision to return to the deep swamp and spend the few remaining years of his life in a world still untouched by progress. Their work had made no difference and the conferences did not stop the devastation. The resolutions of the conferences were always compromises which favored men over animals. There was no hope for the vanishing wildlife, he explained. Their space was being taken away and nothing can live without space.

Dr. Adams had insisted on fighting on and believed there was still a chance to change the morality of man but Madala was tired. As Dr. Adams' old landrover disappeared into the dust of a previously grassy plain, Madala left to make his last mokoro.

The sun was above the forest now and Madala's wrinkled body welcomed its heat. He paddled alongside the mopane forest looking for a convenient place to moor his mokoro. This was the season of the mopane worms which he hoped to collect and dry to give him sustenance at times when the hunt was unsuccessful, which was happening more and more. His eyes had lost their keenness and his stalk its stealth. This reminded Madala he would have to find the larvae of the Diamphidia beetle, to poison his arrows.

Diamphidia. A smile crossed his face as he recalled how much trouble he had remembering this Latin word. Madala wondered if Dr.Adams was still alive and if he still attended environmental conferences. Was he still being criticized for putting wildlife on the same level as human beings? As if God didn't create both, he thought with bitterness. Was he still being asked if humans must suffer to preserve other species?

It was mainly the politicians who asked these questions while they lived in opulence and promoted policies which ensured their extravagant lifestyles and at the same time ensured suffering of the masses. For their seat of power usually acquired by deviousness or brute force, they were prepared to sacrifice all wildlife in the Okavango, or Africa, or the world. And they were.

Despite his hard-headedness, Dr.Adams was losing the battle to which he dedicated his life. Perhaps he would have been happier if he just lived in the wild and left the world to its own course. Madala nearly laughed at the irony. He was the one who had left.

Madala spotted a good place to moor and pushed the mokoro through the grass which grew alongside the shore. He beached the craft, put the quiver on his back, and took the diggingstick in case he found a marula tree on which the Diamphidia beetle feed, and next to which they buried their larvae. He carried his spear in his right hand and slowly walked into the forest, alert to danger.

It wasn't long before he saw little white eggs from which tiny caterpillars of the emperor moth wriggled to feed on mopane leaves. He looked up, saw hundreds of yellow, red and white colored, fully grown and nutritious mopane worms and filled the skin pouch which hung from his shoulder. He was about to go and look for a marula tree when he heard a slow, familiar, movement in the grass and knew he had found supper.

The tortoise pulled in its head and legs when Madala approached, futilely trying to hide inside its shell. Madala twisted a few stalks of long grass together and pushed them in-between the body and the shell so he could carry the tortoise alive and keep the meat fresh. Madala would roast the tortoise in its shell that evening and he looked forward to eating the tender meat cooked in its own juices. His body needed less and less food as age slowed it down, so the tortoise would provide sustenance for a day or two.

He had been thinking about death more and more often, accepting that it was near and natural. He didn't fear death, but he did fear dying before he found the Great Spirit and peace. He sometimes doubted he would ever find the Spirit again. He often thought of the story of God Nyambi, who was once a mortal. Nyambi was so irritated by the continuous dissatisfaction of his people that he had asked the spider Divini to spin him a web to heaven, and once there he had severed the web and cut himself off from the ordinary world.

Madala had always believed the story, but his dealing with the white man had persuaded him that the story was childish. Now he saw clearly how foolish it had been to forsake his beliefs for the beliefs of the white man. The message of the legend was so clear.

Wasn't it dissatisfaction with what he had had, that had made him help the hunter slaughter crocodiles? Wasn't it dissatisfaction with what he had done that made him work with Dr. Adams? Wasn't it dissatisfaction with the lack of success at stopping devastation, that had made him sever ties with his own kind? Wasn't it unhappiness with the absence of peace, that had driven him on the present journey without an aim, except maybe to find a place to die?

For days Madala had had a nagging feeling that there was something he should be doing. He was driven forward, unable to shake his uneasiness.

He put the tortoise upside down on the floor of the mokoro so it wouldn't walk around and pushed the mokoro away from the shore. After a while the swamp changed and he was now travelling through the grass that grew in the shallow waters. He chose his way carefully, moving between little islands from one patch of water to another. Madala saw the crocodiles absorbing the heat of the late morning sun, the same heat that caused his forehead to moisten. Soon, he would have to find a place to rest until the sun lost some of its intensity.

The tortoise was struggling and Madala watched it suffer in the heat, its world turned upside down. He took pity on the creature and turned it over.

The tortoise waited a few minutes before its wrinkled neck cautiously emerged from the shell, then the legs came out and it walked towards the front of the mokoro. Its beaked head moved from side to side looking for a way out. When the tortoise reached the prow it tried to climb out of the mokoro but the angle was too steep. It struggled to climb the side of the mokoro repeatedly and as if eventually realizing that there is no way out the tortoise pulled its head and legs back into its shell and stood still.

Did the tortoise know it was going to die soon, Madala wondered? Was its spirit as heavy as his? Had it given up hope and accepted its fate? Would the acceptance bring peace? Madala watched the tortoise and with sudden clarity he understood that there was no difference between the two of them. He was as trapped by his body and mind as the tortoise was trapped by the sides of the mokoro. The only difference, Madala thought, was that the tortoise had not sinned but had lived life according to its basic survival need. He had perverted his need and demanded more than was his due. He had also given up and accepted that the end of his world and his own end was near. Acceptance didn't bring *him* peace.

Madala directed the mokoro to the shore. As soon as he moored he picked up the tortoise and put it onto the grass. This time its head and legs appeared without hesitation and the tortoise slowly ambled into the thick grass.

Madala felt better, his spirit lightened by his deed. He sat against a tree and closed his eyes. Never before had he deliberately released his prey. Letting the tortoise go, he knew, didn't make a great difference in terms of conservation. He knew that he would have to kill again, but releasing the tortoise had brought a sense of peace which flowed through his body and lightened the burden he had carried for so long.

The tortoise's acceptance of helplessness had touched his heart and he had understood the agony of being on the floor of the mokoro better than he ever understood any other being. To the tortoise he was the Spirit controlling its fate and for the first time he grasped the responsibility of being a man. The release from guilt he had felt when he had let the tortoise go was a reward from the Spirit of the swamp. He sank into a deep relaxing sleep, even though his senses stayed attuned to the surroundings.

As afternoon advanced and the heat subsided, Madala, rested, continued his journey. The swamp was changing again and he navigated the mokoro through the channels in the papyrus. Late that afternoon he spotted the shyest creature of the swamp, the Sitatunga. It lived only in the floating papyrus beds to which it was perfectly adapted. Its extraordinary long and supple hooves supported the antelope's body on the unstable papyrus with ease. She was an excellent swimmer and when threatened she could submerge keeping only her snout outside the water. As she stood erect smelling the wind Madala admired her long twisting horns which pointed backwards reaching almost to her rump.

The mokoro scraped against the stalk of the papyrus and the Sitatunga glanced at Madala, jumped and vanished. The channel along which Madala was travelling led near the spot where he had seen the Sitatunga and he tried to see her again. He didn't see the papyrus moving, as it would if the Sitatunga had run away. Silently he pushed the mokoro in the direction of the place where the Sitatunga had disappeared, but he couldn't sight it. His judgement was wrong, or his old eyes had deceived him he decided, and was about to continue when he saw a stream of blood snaking through the water. He followed the red trail and as he passed a clump of papyrus he saw the Sitatunga held in the jaws of an enormous crocodile. The death was swift.

Although he knew that this was the way of nature, the Sitatunga's death filled Madala with despair. It was so final, he thought. He prayed to the Spirit of the swamp to accept the Sitatunga's spirit and as his mind reached towards the Great Spirit he became aware that there would be no one to pray for his soul when he died.

When he saw the mokoro the crocodile swam away pulling the Sitatunga, her head trailing behind, her open eyes pleading with Madala.

Blood flowed south creating patterns in the crystal clear water at which Madala gazed transfixed. The impact of the Sitatunga's pleading stare smashed the barrier in his soul and the clear message invaded an open mind.

"*You have to go back.*"

Confusion vanished and Madala knew his mission. He was wrong and Dr.Adams was right. There is hope until death takes it away. The tortoise had not died by his hand. Awed by the clarity of his thought and with resolve attained only from a definite objective, Madala turned south following the last traces of blood, one with the Spirit again.

5

The construction of the raft was simple. Rurik made grass ropes and tied the papyrus into cylindrical bundles. Those were in turn tied together. Across the base they laid another layer of bundles to give the raft height, and tied more along the edge for added comfort and security.

In the afternoon of the second day they lowered the raft into the water. It looked beautiful! Proudly Kito took it for a test drive. The raft performed well.

"Now we can travel in style," were Kito's first words as he climbed onto the platform, beaming. Rurik shook his hand.

"Well done, my son. Now we can travel! Let's prepare for the journey," he said smiling.

They rolled the smoked meat in long grass bundles and loaded all their possessions onto the raft. The difficult part was lowering Rurik, but Kito's good balance and a rope made the operation a success. Kito erected the tent and then untied all the ropes that had held the platform together. They ate some of the roast crocodile meat left from lunch and that night they slept on the raft.

Before sunrise they were on their way. Kito was paddling eagerly and seemed to have forgotten that they were lost. This trip was finally becoming the adventure that they had planned. They pushed hard through the reeds and soon found themselves in a channel, probably made by the hippopotamus. Rurik hoped this was an abandoned one; he knew that hippos killed more people in Africa than any other animal. As they turned south the sun rose over their island. In some places the channel narrowed to the width of the raft and they had to pull themselves along until it widened again. Each of the many islands they passed looked similar, with palm trees in abundance. Occasionally they would spot a fish eagle suspended in the sky riding the air currents, a white 'V' adorning its chest, in contrast to the dark feathers on the rest of its body.

For hours they travelled, observing the swamp around them and learning. The channel twisted and turned and sometimes their world was reduced to a patch of sky and papyrus stalks until the channel widened again.

As the sun rose Rurik realized that they needed some kind of protection or the sun would kill them. They decided to stop at the first accessible island to cut four poles with which they could support the tent cover as a sunshade. The first channel which led towards the island opened into a lagoon where twenty hippo were enjoying the shallow waters and mud.

They approached the next island with caution. It looked clear but Rurik knew that in the bush an untrained man observes about ten percent of the life that observes him.

The branches of the trees were hanging low above the water and provided an ideal resting place. For a long time they sat, watching for any sign of danger. Impatience could cost a life and they had the time, Rurik reasoned. Their untrained eyes spotted nothing dangerous.

Kito eventually stood up and stretched, "Dad, it looks clear. I am going."

"Be careful, Kito."

Cautiously, Kito walked through knee deep water with the axe in hand. He reached the land, looked back once and disappeared into the bush. Rurik waited for Kito to return and worried. He listened for sounds that might mean danger for Kito but he heard only the usual sounds of the swamp.

Then a noise startled Rurik. Something big was moving through the bush. He tensed and shifted the focus of his vision in the direction of the approaching sound. His heart pumped faster, but Rurik sat still, feeling helpless and inadequate. Should he warn the boy? If he called, Kito would respond and whatever was in the bush would be alerted to their presence.

From the thicket a massive black head emerged, sniffing the air. Emotionless, the buffalo looked at Rurik, its curved horns held high. Only the shallow water separated Rurik from one of the most unpredictable animals of the African bush. There was no pattern to a buffalo's attacks. Menacingly, the animal stood as if making a decision.

Rurik, an impotent wreck, was afraid to move and unable to fight. He could hardly contain the frustration and humiliation which had built up since the crash because of his inability to perform even basic physiological functions without the help of his son. He felt the blood rush into his head. Madness took over and all reason was gone. He screamed. It was a scream of rage and frustration, a scream of defiance. The buffalo flicked his ears as if chasing away this terrible sound, pivoted on his rear legs, and ran back in the direction from which he had come.

For the first time in five days Rurik felt as if he had performed a manly act. He heard Kito running through the bush. He was being careless again. With axe in hand and worry on his face, Kito burst out of the bush. When he saw Rurik smiling he stopped. "Dad, what's wrong? Why did you scream?" he asked breathlessly.

"There was a buffalo and I scared him away." Rurik said with pride in his voice. It felt good to know that even crippled, he was not helpless. The encounter with the buffalo reminded him that not only physical ability, but also spirit makes a winner or loser.

"You scared a buffalo away by shouting?" Kito asked incredulously. "What if he had attacked?"

"If he had attacked I would probably have been dead by now. I didn't plan to scream; it came by itself."

"I found some good supports. I'm going to get them."

"Kito, be careful. The buffalo might still be in the vicinity," Rurik said apprehensively.

"A buffalo cannot climb trees, and I can also shout." Kito smiled and walked back into the bush.

"Bring some wood on the way back," Rurik shouted.

Rurik watched the spot where his son entered the bush. He had to pay more attention to teaching Kito about survival. The episode with the buffalo had highlighted Rurik's vulnerability. The guidance he gave to Kito could be his testament. He tried to work out the essential values that would guide Kito through the trials of life but found it difficult to summarize the basics of existence.

Kito came back with four straight poles and some fire wood. They erected the sunshade, made a mud fireplace, and secured the cooking pot with a piece of rope long enough to allow them to scoop water.

"Did you think the buffalo would run away when you shouted?" asked Kito once they were back in the channel.

"No, I don't know what made me shout, it just came out. Sheer terror!"

"A big boy like you and scared as a baby," Kito teased.

"One doesn't have to be ashamed of fear. We all fear something. Fear is a defense mechanism. It makes us careful and drives us in times of need. A hero is not a man that has no fear, but a man that overcomes his fear. A man that has no fear is a fool. Where would you place yourself?" Rurik asked, carefully watching his son.

"Sometimes I am afraid," Kito said with a naughty smile.

"Judging by the noise you make while walking through the bush you don't seem to be afraid enough. I hope you appreciate that besides being a real adventure, this is also an adventure of the mind," Rurik said hoping to provoke a question.

"What is an adventure of the mind? But please not a long story!"

Rurik smiled. "If you walk in the streets of a familiar town ..."

"It is a long one again," Kito frowned, but Rurik continued unconcerned.

"... many people walk there. They see what you see. From day to day there are certain changes, different people, some new articles in the shop windows. The picture is much the same, no real excitement. It's a standard life. You get bored and start wondering if that is what life is about. So you leave to search for a meaning and a more exciting life. Soon you encounter a jungle. It is unknown to you and you are nervous but you enter. Adrenaline flows through your body, awakening your senses and tuning you into the environment. The path is very narrow and after a while it stops. You re-examine the path. Perhaps you missed an opening. You discover a hidden opening and you walk a new path. It stops, and again you turn back to find another path. This happens many times, but you progress and go deeper and deeper, sometimes very confused and scared about your position. Still, you don't want to go back. Fear and uncertainty make you feel alive like never before. You have experienced the challenge of the adventure and you don't cherish the return to your standard life. It dulls your mind. Suddenly, an untouched glade with a stream of clear water flowing through it opens in front of you. There is no evidence of anybody having been there before. This success encourages you to go and discover more and you walk along the stream. You know there are obstacles ahead, canyons, waterfalls and other barriers, but now you have confidence. Experience has taught you that you can discover something nobody has discovered before and you go on into a new adventure. In short you live an exciting life," Rurik concluded.

"It is a nice story, but what is the moral of this one?" Kito's eyes twinkled.

"There are two morals. The first is that if you use your brain you can overcome any obstacle and reach conclusions which nobody has reached before."

"And the other?"

"You have to take initiative, overcome the challenges of untried paths and not give up at the first obstacle you encounter. Only then, will you be able to rise above the confusion and lack of direction prevalent in today's society. Then you'll be an individual and not just a member of the masses which clergymen call sheep and governments milk like cows." There was a trace of anger in Rurik's voice.

"Did you leave Croatia and came to Africa to look for an adventure?"

"I left Croatia because of communist oppression. Communism doesn't allow you to think. It tells you what is right and what is wrong. Right is what suits the party hierarchy. Communists preach equality, while the minority at the top of the hierarchy live in luxury, and the majority at the bottom struggle for bare necessities."

"Why did the majority of people accept this situation?" Kito asked.

"Because people are afraid of challenges," Rurik answered, anger in his voice.

"So you left."

"Yes, I realized if I didn't I would also become a sheep."

"Was it hard for you to leave?"

"Yes, it is hard to leave your family and your country. It was a heartbreaking and tearful goodbye. My mother cried and for the first time I saw tears in my father's eyes. This was at the time when traditions had started changing. Children were leaving the land searching for a better life in town. Parents were abandoned by youth who visited less frequently as they established a foothold in the new environment. Values were changing and parents tried to adjust. Their security in old age, previously as solid as a rock and guaranteed by tradition that children looked after their aged parents, started to crumble to sand." Sorrow was in Rurik's heart.

"My father and I travelled by train to the junction from which I would take the train to Germany. I will never forget when I saw my father for the last time. Both of us were standing on the step of the last carriage of trains which moved in opposite directions. Both of us were waving. His steely blue eyes were intense, loving and accepting. The trains increased speed and his waving hand blended with the distance, but for a long time I could see the reflection of the late afternoon sun from the steel strap of a cheap watch." Again Rurik stopped talking, coughed, wiped his eyes and stared into the distance.

"And that was the last time you saw your father?" Kito's question was more a statement, as if he wanted to make sure that he had this significant point right.

"Yes. I spent some time in Europe doing odd jobs, but I was not accepted anywhere. I was a foreigner, and as such, an unworthy individual. I had to carry a paper issued by authorities, on which were details of my residence and job, and which I had to produce if stopped by police. There were frequent blockades of areas where foreigners were concentrated and everybody's papers were checked. If you didn't have papers on you, you would end up in a police cell. Most of the foreigners were political and economic refugees from communism. There were restaurants in Vienna which forbade foreigners. If you went into one of these restaurants they would throw you out, irrespective of how well behaved or dressed you were, what your standard of education was or how much money you had. You were a foreigner, had lesser social standing and you were treated like scum." Rurik's face was stony now and his voice hard as he spoke.

"You see my son, again I had no freedom in a free world. I was not measured by my ability or my intelligence, but by my accent. In revenge, I romanced their wives whom they wined and dined in the restaurants to which I couldn't go. The wives appreciated young and strong foreigners. The struggle to maintain their social status sapped their husband's energy and left them largely impotent."

"Wow Dad, that was sweet revenge," Kito exclaimed. He seemed excited that for the first time his dad was talking to him like a man.

Rurik smiled, aware of the milestone he and Kito had just crossed. "Yes my son it was sweet, but revenge shouldn't guide man's life. Revenge is destructive. Man should have aims which are constructive.

"In any case, I couldn't bear being considered a lesser being so I decided to go to South Africa. I was fascinated by books about the wild continent and the adventures it offered. In Africa, I believed, social status wouldn't matter. Your ability to adapt to nature would be what counted. Of course I was young, and I was wrong." Rurik lifted his hands in a gesture of resignation.

"After about two years of doing odd jobs, I started the advertising business. My accent didn't matter then because everybody had some kind of accent. In South Africa the division was by color. I didn't agree with this new division but didn't do much about it either because now *I* was a first class citizen. I have always believed that man should be judged by his ability and the way in which he uses this ability. I used this same measure in my evaluation of people, irrespective of color, sometimes to my peril. By treating people equally I was undermining the system of division by which numerous bureaucrats lived, and which elevated many others way above the level which they would have attained in a free and fair system."

"But hasn't that changed, Dad?"

"Yes it has. The white government ruled by fear. The black government rules by hypocrisy, using the wrongs of the past to justify the wrongs of the present. It promptly empowered black elite adding it to the white and now people black and white, have to support the extravagant lifestyles of the unified uppercrust. The gravy train is twice as long. You see my son, no matter what system of government is in force there is always the elite that believes that they are God's gift to this world and deserve red carpet treatment, on public expense of course."

"But Dad, you are never happy. You didn't like communists, you were not happy with the government in Europe, you think the white government in South Africa was wrong and now you are saying that the black government is wrong too. What kind of government is good?"

Rurik laughed heartily. "Kito you are still going to accuse me of being anti-government, but I am not. We need a government, but a small and efficient government that can co-ordinate the affairs of the nation and uphold law and order. You are still a bit young to understand the state of the world, but let me tell you the way I see it.

Governments are supposed to work for the good of the nation, but today criminals rule the world. People cannot walk the streets anymore for fear of being mugged or killed. They pay taxes to the government to protect them, but they have to spend fortunes on security systems. All over the world politicians are being exposed for bribery and corruption - even presidents and prime ministers. Taxes are being paid for education, but still, people have to dig in their pockets to educate their children. The government is supposed to protect the environment but the environment is being destroyed at an alarming rate, threatening our survival. All of today's governments are inefficient, bloated self-serving bureaucrats. It is accepted as normal that politicians don't keep the promises they make at election time. They spend millions on propagating promises they don't intend keeping. Politicians are making idiots out of people and people are conditioned to go along with it." Rurik spoke with disgust.

"So Dad, if governments are no good and everything is going so badly why don't people do something about it?"

" Oh they will. Tolerance and ignorance, the same as everything else, have their saturation point. One day the people will revolt, cut bureaucracy to size and reduce the control it has over their lives. Governments will have more of a co-ordinating role than real power over the day to day lives of the population. The only real power the government is going to have is the enforcement of law and order, and the protection of the environment. People are going to demand that laws become more basic, so that they can understand them, and justice swifter. They will realize that criminals are draining resources that could be better employed elsewhere. We might have lawyers digging holes for trees instead of trying to find holes in the law, so that criminals could walk free.

"Dad you seem sure that this is how things are going to go."

"Yes I am sure. Only for so long can you manipulate people. Individualism is a strong instinct once aroused by belittlement and man is going to fight for his freedom, be it from government or criminals. It has happened throughout history and it will happen in the future. I don't think we'll have to wait long. I think the law abiding person has just about had enough of supporting bureaucrats and criminals who live in opulence while his quality of life keeps deteriorating."

"Is this why you went to live at Black Rock?" Kito asked. Rurik's eyes acquired a faraway look and for a few minutes he was lost in thought. Kito waited.

"In a way it was," Rurik said. "Unhappiness with the direction of society made me reassess my life. The death of my father was a turning point in my thinking. I loved him dearly, and since leaving Croatia my dream had been to go back with lots of money, so my father could for the first time in his life have everything he wanted. There was never money for him to buy a new suit, elegant shoes or a good watch. I wanted to provide all of this for him. I was too late. He died before I had made enough money. When I did make lots of money that money no longer had the same value for me because I couldn't give a gold watch to my father. I didn't even think what a burden a watch would be for him while working in the fields, worrying about it getting damaged, or lost." A tear slid down Rurik's face and he quickly wiped it away, embarrassed by the weakness his emotion exposed. To cover it up he looked away and up at the branches of the trees which grew at the edge of the island they were passing.

"Suddenly, what I considered to be my ultimate aim, making money, had lost its importance," Rurik blurted out.

"I discovered Black Rock while on holiday with friends. Because of the bay's remoteness I could be alone for days and at times I would experience absolute peace and tranquillity. When I met your mother she suggested we go and live there. I thought it was a good idea, and I wanted to make your mother happy.

I took the risk of selling my business to live the life I thought would bring us happiness. It wasn't an easy decision but I believed I had the ability to deal with any outcome which my judgement might yield." Rurik looked into the distance remembering doubts which made the decision traumatic and then he turned to Kito, his eyes resolute.

"You have to believe in yourself, Kito. Your belief liberates energies to cope with the task you undertake. Your achievements will be directly proportional to the strength of your belief. If you believe you can do it, you will do it. Once you have a dream you must follow it, build a path towards it and achieve physically what you have already accomplished in your mind. The more care you put into developing your plan, the less energy you spend in its execution. Belief is your greatest strength and doubt your greatest weakness. Believe and your destiny will be in your own hands." Rurik stopped paddling for a moment to emphasize this very important point.

"Is our destiny in our hands, now that we are lost in the swamp and you are injured?" Kito asked defiantly.

"Yes it is, as much as the destiny of any man is in the face of natural laws. If we hadn't taken action we would still be on that tree or maybe even dead. We took action and we are making progress, but we have to continue to keep our spirits up, because this journey might be a long and trying one."

Rurik saw Kito's eyes wander over the surrounding papyrus and he knew he was overdoing it a bit with his preaching, but the incident with the buffalo dramatically altered Rurik's view on his life expectancy. Kito would remember at least some of the advice Rurik had given him and he decided to try and provoke Kito into participation.

"Kito, never concentrate on the problem," he continued, "think *beyond* the problem. If you think beyond the problem, subconsciously your mind will find a solution and strengthen your resolve to get there, preventing the problem from clouding your mind and stifling your imagination into accepting defeat as inevitable. Not to think clearly is a sin and for every sin you pay. For some sins you pay immediately, and for others even your children might end up paying."

"Dad I don't understand how not thinking clearly could be a sin. We think what we think. And how would my children pay for my sin?" Confused, Kito looked at Rurik.

"A clear mind makes decisions based on the basic principles of nature. A confused mind doesn't see those principles and as a result makes an unsound decision. The effects of ill-considered decisions create stress, which consumes energy your body needs to regulate itself, impairing its proper functioning. You weaken. If you then have children, they are not as strong and healthy as they could have been had you had no stress. They pay for your sins, the sins of their father. If your sins affect somebody else, people will fight back. Again, this will create stress in you, with the same results."

"What if I had children already? The sin would only affect me." Kito was suddenly becoming antagonistic. This worried Rurik. What was wrong?

"No my son, it would still affect them." Rurik said in a reasoning voice.

"You'll communicate with them under stress and will not listen attentively. You will be distracted by the problem when your wife and child want to talk to you and tell you about their lives. Your inattentiveness will create stress which will make them unhappy and affect their minds and their health. A seed of unhappiness which you have planted in your family will grow, resulting in your tense interaction with society, spreading stress further."

"So a wrong decision makes the whole world unhappy?" Kito was ironic.

"Yes, the wrong way of thinking and following the wrong principles does." Rurik tried to keep his irritation in check.

"The way you are talking, if we make a mistake we can never be happy again. Things only get worse. Isn't there an end to it?"

"Well, there is an end. Resulting suffering forces you to analyze your actions and see your sin. If you repent and don't sin again, with time your stress decreases and your health improves." Rurik still spoke evenly.

"What are the sins you are talking about?"

"There are a lot! But I'll tell you what I consider to be the most common sins which greatly affect our quality of life. For a start, all excess is a sin. If you eat too much your greed leads to fat. It makes you sluggish. Additional weight stresses your bones and your vital organs. The performance of your body is impaired. Your active life is restricted and your health deteriorates. The resulting unhappiness clouds your mind. If you drink or smoke too much your mind is clouded and your health is affected.

Jealousy is another common sin with severe consequences. If you are jealous of other's possessions you try to get what they have. You adopt their needs and they become a burden. You do not direct your life. Others do. Instead of working for essentials you work for things which are superfluous and as a result destroy some more of nature. Another sin. You see, every activity of man's life has the potential for sin and goodness. If you sin your mind becomes saturated with negativity. If you do good you don't have to reminisce about it. Your mind is free to shape your future. I hope you see it is your choice - heaven or hell."

"It seems so simple to live in paradise," Kito commented.

"It is simple. Paradise is within you, not outside.

"What if you have sinned? Can you achieve paradise?"

"Yes, you can, if you sacrifice."

"What do you sacrifice?"

"If you eat too much, you have to suffer hunger until your diet is compatible with your body's needs. The spiral along which you have slid will bring you up again. If you stop drinking or smoking you'll have withdrawal symptoms. You will suffer, but eventually, you will get paid back in health and vitality. If you stop being greedy you'll find that the sweetness of moderation far exceeds the pleasure of gluttony. In all aspects of your life if you do right, your quality of life will improve. You will have peace of mind."

"Do we always know what is right?" asked Kito.

"It is generally easy to distinguish between right and wrong, unless lawyers are involved," Rurik tried to break the tension which was developing on the raft.

Kito pointed to the sky. A fish eagle was diving with its wings folded and disappeared beyond the reeds. Seconds later he appeared again, a struggling fish in his claws.

"What is right there?"

"The survival of the fittest. The fisheagle has to eat, and the fish is its food. This has been going on since before an eagle was called an eagle and a fish was called a fish."

"What about the conservation you are always talking about?" Again Kito was confrontational.

Rurik's voice hardened. "I keep talking about different kinds of conservation. You cannot ask an eagle to conserve, because he only takes what he needs for survival. If there are more eagles in an area than the area can support, the weaker ones are chased away and die if they cannot find an unoccupied area or win it. If a natural calamity, like a drought, reduces the supply of food they will breed less. We only need to conserve because of man. He kills a lion and a crocodile for their skins, kills a rhino for its horn and an elephant for its tusk. Man kills for vanity. Do you know that there was a plan underway to take water out of the Okavango for a diamond mine?"

"I wish they'd taken the water already. Then we wouldn't be stranded in this endless swamp."

"Kito! I am trying to make you aware of human actions which would influence your life. Do you want the world to be like downtown Johannesburg? Do you want your child to see a cheetah or rhino? Well, it won't if the killings continue." Annoyed, Rurik lifted himself on his hands trying to ease the pain in his back by shifting his body.

"There is no value in diamonds, gold or any other precious metal, except in their industrial use. There are enough diamonds and gold in the vaults of the world to last thousands of years, but we still mine them.

We spend energy, construct roads, open new mines and take

space from other species indiscriminately. We pollute the air and water making the world unliveable for many species and ultimately for ourselves. Non compliance with the law of nature is destroying our world."

"What does the law of nature have to do with all this?"

"The law of nature says that all species need space, all have equal rights and all should take from nature only what they need for existence."

"Then man is the only species in the world that doesn't live according to the principles of nature," Kito exclaimed.

Rurik was struck by the truth of Kito's statement. Man was the only species that destroyed. It was such an obvious truth, it never occurred to him to assimilate it. Stunned by the startling discovery it took Rurik some time to collect his wits.

"Yes, man ..." he started saying, when the water erupted right behind Kito and a huge brown body of a hippopotamus surged to the surface. Two swordlike lower tusks framed a cavernous mouth, big enough to cut a man in half.

"Kito, Hippopotamus!" Rurik screamed but it was too late. The huge mouth grabbed the raft and ferociously threw it upwards. Kito flew backwards and splashed into the water next to the hippo and then Rurik hit the muddied water.

Panic numbed Rurik's brain. The muddy water tasted foul. Messages of shock were flooding his brain, panic consuming the air fast. Disorientation increased the panic and when Rurik tried to swim he felt the mud of the bottom.

Kito ... Was he alive? He had to save his son! Rurik's lungs screamed for air. He yanked desperately with his arms and his body moved through the water, away from the mud. Rurik pleaded with God to protect his son and swam frantically, using the last atoms of oxygen left in his lungs. He broke the surface, gasping.

Rurik faced the island and turned toward the splashing. The remains of the raft were being demolished by the enraged hippopotamus. The hippo repeatedly smashed the water with the raft, pieces flew off and floated on the surface. Kito was not there.

Terror stricken, Rurik looked to his right and his desperation deepened. Kito was not there either. He was about to look behind him, the last place where Kito could be, when he heard his son's panicked voice. "Dad!"

"Kito get out!" screamed Rurik when he saw Kito swim towards him.

"Dad, can you swim?"

"Yes, get out."

Kito didn't heed Rurik's words and swam to him. Rurik looked at the hippo again. A piece of the raft was floating away, their cooking pot securely tied to the papyrus bundle. The hippo spat out the remains of the raft and turned its massive head in their direction, his mouth gaping, his rage focussed on them.

"Swim out!" Rurik screamed.

"No. I'll help you!" Kito gripped his right arm.

"No Kito! I can swim, get out! You can help me out when I am in the shallow."

"Dad swim! It's coming!" Kito's eyes were wide open in terror. He yanked Rurik's arm.

"Swim my son, get out," Rurik sobbed.

He jerked his arm out of Kito's grip and roughly pushed him towards the land. They had no chance. Primeval fear gripped Rurik.

"Get out! Get out!" he screamed at Kito who was trying to get a grip on his arm again.

"Dad, I'll help you!" Kito cried.

Rurik lifted his hand to slap Kito across the face, to make him understand, but when he saw Kito's pleading eyes he couldn't do it. The blow might be the last act Kito remembered of him. He transformed the blow into a stroke and glanced over his shoulder. The hippo would get them in seconds.

"Get out Kito." His voice was a prayer now.

Through the reeds on their left another hippo appeared.

"Watch out! Another hippo! Swim! Save yourself." Rurik pleaded with his son.

"Swim Dad! This is a small one!" Kito had a grip on Rurik's arm and was pulling desperately.

Frightened by all the shouting, the baby hippo jumped into the water and waded to his mother. Kito swam frantically using his free arm, his eyes darting backwards. Then he stopped swimming and the fear in his eyes changed to relief and astonishment. Rurik looked back. The mother was pushing her child gently into deeper water, away from danger. The relief was wondrous.

"Let's get out," said Rurik, aware that besides hippos, there might also be crocodiles.

They swam until Kito could stand. Then he pulled Rurik onto a small grassy plain and up a gentle slope into the shade of a huge tree, twenty meters from the water. Hard, spiky grass pierced Rurik's wet trousers and the pain startled him. At first he tried to ignore it, as he had learned to ignore the continuous pain in his back, but then the realization that feeling had returned to his legs penetrated his exhausted mind. He wanted to shout with elation but held back. He had to make sure there was a decisive improvement, before he gave Kito false hope.

When Kito had helped him lean up against the tree, Rurik tried to move his toes. He couldn't, but pain was a good sign. Possibly, in the desperation to get away from the hippo, his brain driven by the survival instinct, had forced the nerves to transmit its instructions and had partially succeeded.

Breathing hard, Rurik gazed at the swamp, the place where they had been only seconds from death, then he turned to look at Kito. The axe and emergency kit hung from the belt on the boy's right hip, the knife on his left and water dripped from his clothing. He looked like a victorious warrior as he stared at the swamp.

Kito turned around to Rurik. "We'll have to build a shelter again," he said.

"And then we'll have to look for food," Rurik added. Survival was becoming a daily chore.

They decided to make a lean-to from saplings and cover it with foliage. Kito brought the materials, Rurik cut saplings to the required lengths and Kito wove them together, constructing a sloping lattice. The higher end was supported by two Y-shaped sticks, while the other end rested on the ground. When the frame was finished, Kito wove long thin branches complete with foliage into the lattice, creating a well covered roof. He collected armfuls of dried grass to use as beds and finally they had a sturdy and cosy space in the shade of a tree, another temporary home.

Kito gathered wood and Rurik made a fire. All they needed now, was food, he thought.

"Maybe you could go and see if you can recover some of our possessions," Rurik said. "I saw a bundle of papyrus with the pot tied to it floating not so far away. Perhaps it has caught in the reeds somewhere. Some rope would help too, we always need rope."

"I'll go later on. First I'm going to rest. I'm tired." Kito's quiet voice made Rurik take a closer look at his son, who sat on a small log. He looked exhausted, beads of sweat thick on his forehead and his eyes old and fatigued. Rurik had noticed the sweat before, but didn't pay any attention because the day was hot and they worked hard.

"Kito are you all right?" he asked.

"I'm okay. I'm just tired and I have a headache. I will see if I can find any of our things." He stood up and walked down the slope, his shoulders stooped. His step was heavy and his hands hung loosely. Anxiety gripped Rurik. Was Kito getting ill? Please God, no. They were in enough trouble already.

""Kito be alert," Rurik called after his son. "If you see the hippopotamus close to any of our things, don't try and recover them. The hippos are not as agile on land as in water, but they are faster than you would think. Keep a safe distance."

"I'll be careful Dad." But Kito entered the reeds carelessly.

There *was* something wrong. Kito shouldn't be so tired, Rurik thought. He must be getting ill. The thought frightened Rurik.

Sudden loneliness, so deep and immense that it left no hope in the soul, overcame him. He looked across the still waters of the lagoon in which a dead tree was reflected and into the deep blue sky. Rurik closed his eyes. Please God, don't let Kito get sick, he prayed fervently. If you are punishing me for my sins haven't I paid the price already? What have I done that is so terrible? Rurik recalled his life and his anxiety grew deeper.

The noise of Kito's footsteps brought Rurik back. Kito emerged from the reeds with the pot in hand and a length of nylon rope trailing behind. His face was drawn, his eyes were glazed, and he walked as if in a dream, detached from the world around him. Alarmed by Kito's appearance Rurik attempted to lift his spirits.

"Well done Kito!"

"Dad, I am really tired and my head feels as though it will split."

Malaria! The thought hit Rurik and overwhelmed his senses. The disease was dreaded throughout the tropics and he knew that even with medicine the chances of survival were slim, unless the disease was identified and treated within two to three days. Bouts of fever occur at regular intervals, alternating with periods of partial recovery leaving its victim too weak to fight.

"Come here son," he said, his body shaking with dread.

Kito sat heavily next to Rurik. His forehead was burning. Perhaps it was some other, less lethal, tropical disease, Rurik thought. But most of them brought delirium. Who would get them food? Without food to give him energy to fight, the boy's chances were infinitesimal. Rurik was bewildered. Was he going to lose his son?

"Kito, you are ill. Lie down and rest. Rest will give your body a chance to fight. Don't forget you are a fighter. You must fight," Rurik's voice shook.

"What about you Dad?"

"I'll take care of you my son. You know that I can take care of us. I always have."

Kito's smile was weak and sad. Rurik could see that he didn't believe that his Dad could do it now. Before the fever took over Rurik had to change Kito's mind. He must believe that they would win, otherwise there was no chance.

"You need to take some anti-malaria tablets. They might help you. Go and get some water and take two tablets."

Kito got up and staggered. He steadied himself and bent to pick up the pot. The small cooking pot was a considerable effort for his strength now. He walked wearily, his will failing. Rurik *had to* help his son.

A heap of foliage was still lying next to the lean-to and Rurik moved to get it. He put his hands on the ground behind him and then dragged his body. The foliage made an uncomfortable pillow and Rurik spread some grass over it.

Kito came back with the water and sat under the lean-to. His suffering was obvious and Rurik suffered with him. He took two tablets out of his emergency kit and gave them to Kito.

Kito lay down and his body relaxed slightly. "What is going to happen to us? he asked, his eyes closed.

"God will help us," answered Rurik, tears forcing their way out of his eyes.

"But why would God put us in this predicament?"

"My son, God is only testing us. Through being tested we learn about ourselves. We discover powers that would elude our understanding were we not forced into the deeper thinking that comes with trials. We are often limited by others' perceptions of human potential and we just take for granted that it is the right perception, because it's an easy way. We don't put ourselves to the test and we perform below our real abilities. Now we are being tested, and we *have to* pass the test."

"Haven't we been tested enough?"

"We always think so, but we don't really know. Sometimes we are slow to learn. But there is one thing you must not forget. Within you there is a force of life that controls you. In your mind you have to give that force a future and it will take you there. There are things you dream of doing. Believe you will do them and your life force will take you there through the ebb and the flow of your power. Your belief will be the anchor for the force of life. This is very important. Do not accept defeat and *we will* travel together again."

Kito opened his eyes and they shone with intensity. Was it the intensity of belief or the intensity of the fever, Rurik asked himself.

Kito fought to stay awake, but eventually he slipped into unconsciousness.

"Fight my son, fight," Rurik repeated, now sobbing freely, hoping his words and feelings would penetrate into Kito's subliminal world.

6

Rurik watched his son's pale face and listened to Kito's labored breathing. He had to reduce Kito's fever.

Rurik cut off his trouser leg below the knee and for hours he sat next to Kito wiping his face with the wet cloth. The pot of water was nearly empty, but Kito's high temperature didn't subside. The African night, filled with uncertainty and menace, was descending fast and already a few stars were visible. Rurik realized that he didn't have enough wood to see him through the night and he moved to gather some. Dead wood was lying in abundance throughout the bush and piece by piece Rurik collected it wiping Kito's face every time he brought wood. By the time he had hoarded enough wood it was completely dark and Rurik was exhausted.

The water was only twenty meters away, but to Rurik the distance represented a great effort as he set off with the cast iron pot. The closer to the water he came the darker it looked. When he reached the shallows his hands sunk into the mud, his trousers got soaked and his fear increased, but he had to get deeper. In the shallows he would scoop mud. When the water was up to his waist he filled the pot. Need and fear drove Rurik and he dragged the heavy pot out of the water and back to the fire.

Kito was shivering so Rurik put some wood on the fire, dried his shirt and put it over Kito. Still Kito shivered.

Miserable, Rurik gazed at the flames playing on the branches above and the bush behind, constantly changing the depth of their world and wondered what to do. The sweat, from the effort of carrying the pot and the heat of the fire, slid down his naked torso, taking excess heat away. This made Rurik aware that there was something he could do.

He snapped out of the melancholy. To drag himself behind Kito and place Kito between himself and the fire was difficult. Lack of headroom at the lower end of the lean-to forced Rurik to claw his way in. The sharp grass cut his fingers and chest. The pain was however, incidental, compared with his need to help his son.

Bleeding, Rurik lay alongside his boy, hugging him and hoping the lower temperature of his body would drain Kito's fever away. Kito had to get better. Any animal that sensed their helplessness would attack. As soon as Kito stopped shivering Rurik would make some sort of weapon. He would fight and die before he let an animal harm Kito.

Rurik lay alongside his son not knowing whether he was harming or helping him, following his instinct and planning his future, however short it might be. He lay hugging his son for a long time before Kito's teeth stopped chattering. Rurik wondered if it was the cycle of the fever or if it was he that made a difference. Just in case he did, he lay alongside his son for a long time.

A piercing howl from the tree above them filled the night. Rurik lay motionless, straining to understand the mysterious night of the Okavango. What could make such a blood-curdling sound? Maybe it was the death scream of a bird as the fangs of a black mamba penetrated its body. The night suited a black mamba. It was dark and evil. Shivers ran down his spine, breaking the rigidity the howl had caused.

Rurik dragged himself out of the lean to and added some wood to the fire. There was a popular belief that wild animals wouldn't approach a fire and Rurik hoped that that belief was justified.

Rurik thought it was time to give Kito another dose of anti malaria tablets. Judging by the speed with which the fever had overtaken Kito's system, the attack was massive and it required an intense concentration of medicine to stop it and turn it back, Rurik reasoned.

He couldn't put the tablets directly into Kito's mouth for fear of him choking. With cupped hands he scooped water from the pot, filled his mouth, tilted his head backwards and dropped two antimalaria tablets into the water. The bitterness froze Rurik's mouth and forced tears to his eyes.

He resisted the temptation to spit out the bitter liquid with the willpower of a desperate man. Those two tablets were twenty percent of their medicine. When he thought that the tablets had melted, Rurik forced Kito's mouth open and then carefully poured the liquid down his throat.

Kito coughed, spewing some of the liquid out, but he swallowed most of it. His temperature seemed to be getting lower and hope filled Rurik's soul. Maybe it was just sunstroke, he thought. Maybe Kito would be okay in the morning. They could make another raft and continue their journey, and he would have his son back. It was so lonely, and without Kito there was no future.

Beads of sweat soon formed on Kito's forehead, and dark thoughts suppressed hope and deepened Rurik's misery. For hours he sat next to Kito wiping his forehead. Kito was losing too much fluid and would become dehydrated. Why hadn't he thought about it before? Rurik filled his mouth with water then poured the water into Kito's.

Beyond the reach of the flames the darkness was dense and constantly threatened their small flickering world. He must save on wood, he thought. It had to last at least until the moon rose. It would be better to have a smaller fire all night than risk running out of wood. Tomorrow, he would make sure there was enough wood.

"Dad, I am falling!" Kito's scream startled Rurik. "Dad, help me, I am falling!" His hands were reaching, trying to find Rurik. Rurik grabbed Kito's hands and held them firmly.

"You will not fall, my son. I will hold you. You will not fall, my son," Rurik repeated.

"Dad please, I am falling!" Kito's voice was frantic. He tried to get up, but Rurik held him down.

"Kito, there is no end to the fall. You must not get to the end. There is a line. Find it. It is within you. Look my son, look. Do not let the end come. The end is far away. Catch the line. Fight Kito, fight." Rurik was hugging his son, his cheek against Kito's, his mind reaching for Kito's.

"Dad! Dad! Please Dad, help me!" Kito's screams tortured Rurik's soul. Only God could help him. "Please God give me the power to join my mind with my son's. Let us break the fall together," he whispered.

"God forgive me. You are my only option. Please help me. Bring my son back," Rurik pleaded.

Two pictures flashed through his mind simultaneously, bringing into focus a common point; love. The first, Rurik under the murky water unable to swim until the thought of his son had given him strength. The other, the attacking hippo stopping its pursuit to guide its child to safety. Love had saved his life twice within minutes. But how could love help his son now? Rurik's mind raced. Love leaves no place for impure thoughts. He could purify his mind with love. Only a pure mind could reach the ultimate mind.

Forlorn, Rurik focussed on Kito's pale and lifeless face. Kito was near the end. Tears clouded Rurik's vision and sobs tore his soul. The fire reflected through his tears and created images of stars twinkling on his son's still face. His sobs became deeper. For an eternity he sat next to his boy, his tears exhausted and his sobs spent, leaving immense emptiness.

Gently Rurik stroked Kito's face, wishing he would sweat again or scream with a nightmare. Anything was preferable to Kito lying unmoving, the only sign of life an almost imperceptible, irregular, rising of his chest.

Rurik had to do something. He couldn't just sit waiting for Kito to die. He could give him two more tablets, but the pot was empty again. He put a few more pieces of wood on the fire to light his way, and started towards the water. This time the pot seemed heavier. He crawled down the slope. Now his fear of the swamp was only instinctive. The fear for life was gone.

When Rurik filled the pot it was too heavy. He poured out some water and with the pot half empty, slowly moved up the slope. He was about to enter the shadow of the tree when the water spilled. He was careless and the tear in his pants had hooked the ear of the pot and it had overturned.

He would have to go back again, but first he had to rest. He lay on his back. Half the sky was full of stars, the other half hidden by branches.

* * * *

Rurik lay on his back and stared at the myriad stars of the milky way encircling the heavens. Mesmerized by the breathtaking beauty, Rurik reminded himself that he had to get water and go to his son. He would rest for a few more minutes and then he would go, he thought while he gazed at the mysterious sky.

His mind was drawn into space and he felt his senses responding to the vibrations of the universe and his resignation draining along its waves until in a hypnotic state his intellect permeated space and time, and he saw an incredible picture of harmony.

Countless galaxies travelled on predetermined paths at incredible speeds. The worlds orbited around the stars, tranquil and natural, and on many he perceived life.

Then he saw a speck of dust surrounded by a blue haze, hurtling through space and his mind focussed on this intriguing blue glow.

The beautiful blue planet filled his vision and he saw life being created patiently, in perfect balance, over billions of years, by the unimaginable powers of nature.

Rurik saw the rhino with his family, his mate and his offspring in this natural world. The unhurried clock of nature ticked and for a hundred and fifty million years the rhino lived undisturbed, in perfect harmony with laws of nature.

Then an ape, in a battle for choice fruit, grabbed a stick and bludgeoned another ape to death. He stood on two legs and let out a terrible scream of victory, frightening blood-lust in his eyes. The ape walked tall, and to confirm his power he destroyed everything in his path. Rurik saw the world of the rhino being annihilated by this ruthless creature who learned how to make more and more tools of destruction until he was stronger than the rhino. The rhino retreated with his mate and his child, but the destruction continued. The rhino retreated further and the ape, by now a monster obsessed with self-importance, destroyed relentlessly.

The ape's inner strength became drained by the wasteland he had created and his only power rested with the weapons of destruction. Denying his inner weakness, the ape created mayhem in the zeal to prove that he reigned supreme. The rhino's world vanished and the last rhino died. The two legged creature, aware of the loss of his inner power, and afraid that others would see it too, hacked off the rhino's magnificent horn. Secretly he ground it into dust and drank the powder in the mistaken belief that this symbol of the rhino's manhood would reinstate the potency he had lost.

Rurik saw the wave of deception sweeping the world, ravaging man and nature alike. The world of the rhino was destroyed by a man who had tried to regain his virility from the rhino's powdered horn. Rurik recognized the futility of this attempt as man failed to look inward and correct what is wrong.

He saw the universe rotate according to the law of God. He saw life being created and censured according to that law. He saw that the road along which mankind walked disregarded the basic concepts of this law and his inquisitive mind followed the road into the future, then terrified recoiled back, past the present, and it stopped in the tranquil world of Rurik's youth. He was a child again.

Rurik and his father sat in the shade of an oak tree. A cool breeze made the heat of the summer day bearable. Bread, cheese, smoked bacon and onion looked appetizing and welcome after a morning of scything wheat.

Through the shimmering haze Rurik looked down the valley where the wheat was swaying in the breeze. It hung heavy with seed.

"It is beautiful. Is it not?" his father said. "This season we are blessed. The harvest will be rich."

Rurik's father's steely blue eyes were tranquil and reassuring. His bronzed face, weathered from many days in the sun, gave Rurik comfort and security. They spent all year in the fields, digging the vineyard, planting maize, planting and harvesting onions, beans, peas and potatoes; and taking care of a multitude of other necessities. It required many days in the sun to be self-sufficient. The whole family had to work.

"Father, why do we have to work so hard?" Rurik asked. He didn't like the idea of going back into the sun, where the leaves of the wheat and burrs would stick to his sweaty skin.

"My son, we have to work. We have to prepare sustenance for our family. The winter is coming and if we don't have food we will have to beg and be at the mercy of others. To me death would be preferable."

Rurik couldn't imagine his father beg. He remembered the old woman dressed in black woollen clothes of mourning, summer and winter. The Serbs had killed her husband and four sons in the war and there was nobody to work the fields. She would squat by their door and pray, looking so weak, vulnerable and helpless. His grandmother always gave her a piece of bread, and sometimes, in a good year, a piece of cheese or bacon. The woman would praise God and move next door to pray. On her back, bent by age and misery, she carried a woollen bag. The more pieces of bread she got, the heavier the bag became. Rurik often wondered after how many doors the burden became too heavy. No, he couldn't imagine his father beg.

"I know, but there are people who do not have to work the fields and have a much better life. We are always in the sun or the rain, dust or mud," Rurik complained.

"We also walk on a carpet of flowers in spring and breathe rich and clean air after the rain. My son, every kind of life has its burdens and happy moments. Life is a challenge and a challenge is never easy. It is a series of tests and the more tests you pass the more your life will be what you want it to be. One day perhaps you will want what you have now, but remember what you have had you cannot have again. Otherwise, you would be trapped in time and an unchanging mind." His father's gaze shifted and wandered over the fields, his expression was one of quiet appreciation.

"You must follow your dream and learn by your mistakes. It won't be easy, but accept the challenges and build the steps towards your dream. The steps may be difficult to build, but if you do not persevere there is always going to be an unbridgeable abyss between you and your goal. There will often be apparently easy ways. Think well before you take them. Sometimes beware. What you are taught may not be true. Always do what you believe is right." Rurik's father took a deep breath and squared his shoulders.

"But do not ever forget the land. Land gives life, and it is blessed. You plant one seed of wheat and ten will be given back to you in a sheaf. You plant one fruit tree and harvest fruit for many years. Do not forget this. When you get confused about your direction, remember the land and it will show you the principles by which nature works. Knowledge will come with it, make you strong and give you security in times of doubt, it will give you a clear path. The steps will be there. Learn from nature. It is an honest teacher."

Rurik tried to understand, but some of it he couldn't understand. Often he had to think about his father's words to understand them. His father always made him think. Rurik first realized that when his father spoke to him about the mountains.

"As you progress through the mountains you always see them from one side," his father had said. "To remember your way back, you have to turn around and see each mountain from the other side as you pass. On the return journey you will not get lost. You also have to note the position of the sun because from a different angle the sun shades the cliffs and valleys differently. The same mountain can look beautiful, dangerous or treacherous. Your perception of beauty or danger is dependant upon your position."

Only afterwards Rurik realized that his father wanted him to understand that everything contained both good and bad and it was his choice which one to select. Rurik was thirteen now and wanted to show his father that he understood what his father was saying, but he didn't really. He closed his eyes to concentrate. Why couldn't man have what he had had before and how would he be trapped by time and an unchanging mind? It didn't make sense.

Rurik opened his eyes to argue but his father wasn't there anymore. He was fading into the distance, a rifle in his hand and a rucksack over his shoulders.

"Father come back," Rurik shouted.

"My son I have to go." His voice boomed from the distance.

"Don't go Father. You cannot leave me alone. There is still so much I don't understand."

"Life will teach you, my son. I must go. The Serbs are mutilating and killing our people and burning our homes again. We have to stop them. If we don't they will annihilate us. They want our land and only our courage and determination will stop them."

"Please stay," screamed Rurik as he saw the first dark clouds appear on the horizon.

"My son I have no choice. I have to defend our home and our family, otherwise we will be dead or slaves to the savages. I have to go. Face bravely every challenge you encounter. That is the only life worth living."

The black clouds were coming in fast. A terrible storm was brewing. How was he going to survive the storm with his father gone?

He understood why his father had to go. He had told Rurik what the Serbs did in another war. They raped children and women, gauged eyes, mutilated the innocent and sowed terror to frighten people off their own land. Rurik had asked his father why their ancestors gave sanctuary to people like the Serbs and then allowed them to settle in their land. His father answered that their ancestors had lacked foresight. In doing what they thought to be humane, giving protection to people that were running away from the Turks, they had made a mistake. Now their descendants were paying for the sins of their fathers.

The clouds, driven by furious winds, enveloped his father's face. Only the steely eyes were penetrating the gloominess. The gust of wind rolled the cloud away, and it was the calm wise face of his grandfather Rurik saw. With each new gust the face changed but the steel of the eyes remained the same. Each new face he glimpsed through the rolling clouds was further in the past, each more shrouded in the mist, each more mysterious than the one before. Then there was no face and no change, as if the visions had reached back to the beginning of time. There were just those beautiful eyes. Strong winds drove the clouds furiously, threatening to envelop the vision and cut Rurik off.

The eyes beamed peace through the mist, compelling him to accept his destiny. But Rurik was scared because he had to face the future alone. Acceptance was hard, but looking at the eyes, Rurik realized that he never was truly alone.

A bolt of lightening flashed across the sky blinding him and almost immediately he heard thunder. When he regained his sight, Rurik looked for the eyes, but the eyes were gone.

"Father do not abandon me," he screamed into the mist and his desperate scream blended with the terrible scream from above. It was the blood-curdling scream he had heard in the night and in the silvery moonshine he recognized a Pels fishing owl and then he saw the eyes again. The eyes of the owl.

Kito! Rurik felt remorse. He had to get water.

Still dazed by the illusion Rurik lifted himself up and looked back to where Kito was lying. The fire had nearly burnt out, its flames too small to see clearly, moonshine blocked by the boughs of the tree. Kito looked changed and was moving in a strange way. Rurik's eyesight adjusted to the flickering of the fire and his senses reeled from shock.

A python was curling itself around Kito. Rurik scrambled. His fingers dug into the earth like the spikes of a fork, and he dragged his body along the ground frantically.

He had to go for the neck. Cut the oxygen off. Strangle. Could he kill the snake? He knew that the only solution was to kill, be killed or let Kito be killed. As he came closer, he saw the snake was huge.

The snake's head was near Kito's chin. Rurik grabbed the python's neck, but didn't seem to make any difference. The snake felt as hard as a fire-hose with water at high pressure going through it. He *had to* move it. The snake continued to curl itself around Kito's body. His sweaty face was contorted in pain. Rurik's mind was racing, there was not much time. He had to move the snake before it was too late, before Kito was crushed.

Rurik tugged repeatedly and the snake's head turned in his direction. The cold eyes looked at Rurik's. In them he saw the calm acceptance that survival constantly requires a struggle. Rurik's eyes became as cold as the snake's. It was going to strike and Rurik had to make it miss.

The snake curled back into an 'S', pulling Rurik along. The strike was coming. Only by co-ordinating his mind and body did Rurik have a chance of success. He knew that even the lower part of his body must be used, if only as weight. When the snake struck he would have to simultaneously move his body to one side and his head to the other.

Rurik put the scheme into action as the snake struck toward his head. There was no way of stopping the snake; its power was enormous. Rurik held onto the snake as his body was thrown backwards. He landed on his back next to the fire and held on as the python rolled him around, trying to get out of the stranglehold.

Rurik's body rolled to and from the fire at the whim of the snake.

Adrenaline flowed, increasing Rurik's strength and he squeezed vigorously. He felt the grass cutting his bare back and the wetness of blood. The snake started uncurling itself from Kito. Now he would have to deal with all of the massive body. He must not panic. He had to face the reptile without fear, otherwise he would die and so would Kito.

Rurik felt the pressure around his waist as the snake unhurriedly coiled itself around his body. The pain in his back increased dramatically. Rurik smelt burning cloth and then a searing pain shot from his ankle.

The snake curled itself around his chest, rolling him around like a log. Rurik's ribcage closed around his lungs squeezing out the air. He squeezed. There was not much time left. The snake squeezed. As more air left Rurik's lungs a black cloud formed on the periphery of his consciousness; threatening to smother his senses. Strangely he accepted it as a relief. It would bring an end to this unbearable pressure. Only atoms of air were left. Rurik closed his eyes.

"God forgive me for my sins." Blackness was invading Rurik's mind fast and he knew it was over.

Then through the darkness he heard a voice. It was booming through his universe.

"Do not give up. Accept the challenge and fight!"

He flashed back the message.

"But father how? You didn't give me enough strength." Intense and stern steely eyes pierced the darkness.

"I did. You wasted it. *Do not give up.*" Rurik's father was angry. Rurik had wasted the power he had given him by his impure thoughts. Recognition that he could not elude the unimaginable anticipation of natural laws shattered his belief that wicked thoughts wouldn't be punished. They destroyed the soul and sapped power. In an instant he confessed his sins.

"Father, please forgive me. *I will change my ways,*" his mind flashed.

The eyes changed. They were not hard anymore and shone with

love. Rurik, the prodigal son was accepted back. He had confessed, repented and was forgiven.

Lightning flashed out of the eyes and when it reached Rurik, strength flowed into his body. With his left hand he held the snake's neck, and with his right he reached for the knife. The neck was slipping away. Rurik pulled the knife out of its sheath and with all his power he struck the neck. The pressure on his body increased and then relaxed as the snake's muscles slackened in death.

Rurik disentangled himself from the coils of the snake, hurried to Kito and sunk to his knees to hug his son. Kito was still alive. They had won.

Elated, Rurik wanted to scream and then, stunned, he lost his breath. He could walk again! Disbelief swept away all other emotions and Rurik jerked himself upright. His eyes wide open, in amazement he looked at his legs. Then slowly, as if he was afraid that the illusion would evaporate, he lifted his left leg and placed his foot on the ground. Hesitantly he stood up. His legs shook and the pain in his ankle, momentarily suppressed by the surge of emotions, came back. He looked at the source of the pain which had told him that he was whole again and saw the bottom part of his trouser leg was burnt away. The end was still smoldering. Just above his ankle the skin was burnt away leaving an ugly black patch. Neither pain nor weakness in his legs could diminish his elation. He could take care of Kito again. He was not powerless. He was a whole man again, enriched by the incredible experience of divine intervention.

Questions flashed through Rurik's mind. How did this happen? How had he been cured? The nerves in his spine must have been stunned. The pressure of the snake and his superhuman effort must have forced his nerves to function again. He had heard of miracles like this before, when an event made people who couldn't walk for years, walk again, or a mother lift a car off her child. Mysterious were the ways of the Lord!

Humbled, Rurik sank to his knees again. The snake lay before him. Their paths had crossed in the battle for survival and Rurik mourned its death. The snake was not his enemy. His interaction with the snake had given him an understanding he had not possessed before, the understanding of the continuity of life. He understood who his father was, and his fathers' father, and his son's father. Gently he pulled the knife out of the snake's neck and wiped it on his trouser leg. The incision in the snake's neck was almost invisible and it now looked as if it were sleeping. Rurik put the knife back into its sheath.

He looked at Kito breathing heavily, drops of sweat thick on his forehead. He had to get water. Rurik filled the pot up and full of hope, he carried it with ease. A hint of light came from the eastern horizon. A new day was being born and there was certainty in Rurik's step.

7

For hours Rurik wiped the sweat from Kito's face, and by midmorning Kito's breathing had normalized and his perspiration was reduced. The hope that his son was getting better lifted Rurik's spirits further.

He had tried to wake Kito a few times and share his excitement with his son, sure that the knowledge that they were not helpless would help Kito fight the illness. Impatient, Rurik walked around collecting wood, building a pile big enough for a week. He saw clearly how incomplete any victory was without the ability to share it with somebody who cared. The sun was about half way up when Kito's eyelids fluttered for the first time, making Rurik's heart jump with anticipation.

"Kito. Wake up." He gently patted his son's face.

Slowly Kito's eyes opened.

"Kito, it's me, Dad! Wake up son!"

Recognition cleared the dullness in Kito's eyes and his lips moved soundlessly.

"Kito, I am so happy you are awake." Rurik held Kito's hands in his and squeezed them gently.

Again Kito's lips moved and this time a barely audible sound came out. "Dad, I am so tired."

"You will be fine. You have just come through a fever attack. You are a strong boy and I am very proud of you. You are a real fighter and you have fought bravely. I also have very good news for you. I can walk again." Rurik didn't have to force excitement into his voice.

"You can walk!" Kito lifted his head up a little but then he sunk back, the effort making him breathe hard.

"Yes, my son, I can walk. I can take care of you now. We'll be fine."

"That is fantastic! How did it happen? Kito was fully awake now, excitement restoring his energy fast.

"A miracle happened. I fought a python and in the process I regained the use of my legs. My spine probably wasn't badly damaged and I suppose, as the swelling went down, things were coming back to normal. When I fought the python I was forced to use all my energy and my body responded."

"You fought a python?" Kito asked incredulously. "Where is it now?"

Rurik stood up and moved away so Kito could see the snake.

"There." He pointed to the massive, intricately painted coils of the snake that lay alongside the fire.

"It's huge! Kito tried to lift himself on his elbows, to see better, but he was still weak and could only turn his head. "How did you manage to kill it? It's a monster."

"My son so many things happened last night that I don't know where to start. The only thing I can tell you with certainty is that deep within us there are powers that we don't understand and don't even know exist. Last night it was revealed to me that laws that govern not only our lives, but the universe as well should be understood and obeyed. By understanding these laws our own empowerment increases proportionally to our compliance. I was able to win the battle because I was made to see clearly some basic truths, and as a result I received power I didn't possess before."

"I don't understand what you are talking about. How did you receive power that you didn't have before?" Kito frowned in puzzlement, his confusion apparent.

"I know it is all very confusing, even for me. I did have power, but I didn't know how great it was until it was freed by a blend of deep desperation and love. I love you. And that was all that mattered last night. My love gave me the power which wasn't there before."

"But I thought you always loved me," Kito said, baffled.

"Yes Kito. Of course I have always loved you, but last night you were very sick and I thought I was going to lose you ..." Rurik hugged his boy and Kito responded by weakly embracing Rurik's shoulders.

"I am so happy that you are better. I was so worried." Rurik tried to keep his voice level. "Now that you are well, you need to eat. I am going to cook some of the python's meat and I am going to smoke some. You rest."

"Okay. But have you eaten snake meat before? I wonder what it tastes like." Kito said, contemplating the coils of meat.

"No, I have never eaten snake meat, but we have both eaten eel. I believe it has a similar taste. We'll have to find out, won't we? The menu we have is quite limited. Snake." Kito's laugh was the best sound Rurik had heard in his life.

Rurik cut the snake's head off, skinned the part behind the neck and cut pieces of meat to cook in the pot. While the meat was cooking he cut a few saplings to make a smoking platform and at the same time surveyed the area. He discovered an animal path and walked along it, always aware that he might meet the regular users of the path. As he passed the impressive Baobab tree, which legend said, God planted upside down, a clearing surrounded by big trees and thick bush opened in front of him. A small herd of buffalo were grazing at the far end. Two kudu appeared from the bush on the far right and joined the buffalo. Rurik made note of the place and walked back to Kito. By the time he had made the smoking platform the meat was cooked and they ate. The meat was tasteless without salt and Kito complained, insisting that he was not hungry, but Rurik forced him to eat. The snake was so long he struggled to hang it from the branch and when he was finished more than half of it was still on the ground.

While Rurik was skinning the snake he wondered whether he should give Kito two anti-malaria tablets, but decided against it. During last night and the morning he had given Kito six tablets, hoping to contain the fever. Kito looked stronger now sitting against a pile of reeds which Rurik had tied into a bundle. He was even giving Rurik advice about where to hang the meat that couldn't fit on the smoking platform. There was no more space on the branch where the smoke would reach the meat. Rurik dragged the snake into the water hoping that the crocodiles would take it, otherwise, when the flesh started to smell it would attract all kinds of predators, which reminded Rurik that he had to build some kind of protection.

Bent under the weight of the snake he saw his reflection as he entered the water. Half a trouser leg was missing, the other hung in strips. The shirt on his chest was torn, exposing caked blood mixed with hair. One sleeve was gone and only one button held below the belly. His face was dirty. Still, under the rags and surface dirt confidence and determination showed. Rurik dropped the snake into the water and bent to wash his face. He saw his own eyes staring at him resolutely.

Rurik was shocked by the way his clothing looked. New clothing would be unsuitable for the task of building the protective barrier around the camp, he consoled himself. Clothing didn't make a man any different. It just made him look different, he reasoned further. Clothing was another of man's vanities and deceptions, Rurik concluded.

He walked back and decided that thorny bushes would be the most effective barrier. While he dragged dead thorny bushes back to the clearing and arranged them in a circle he could not help wondering if there was any aspect of man's life that had not been affected by vanity. He was still wondering by the time he finished the fence.

The fence was sturdy and the thorny bush looked impenetrable, but Rurik knew he couldn't relax his vigilance. A barrier wouldn't stop a determined and hungry predator sensing weak prey. He made two spears and hardened the tips over the fire. As he leaned them against the fence a movement caught his eye. It seemed that the snake was alive and swimming away, the front of its body submerged, the rest following in a straight line. Rurik waited for the snake to re-emerge, but the surface of the swamp remained placid. He knew that was the last time he would see the creature which had restored his mobility.

Kito lay with his eyes closed. His energy seemed to drain with the falling of the dusk and Rurik was afraid a new attack would come soon. He hoped Kito had enough energy to fight off a new bout of fever. Rurik prepared some snake for supper knowing that he would have to find another source of food to help boost Kito's energy. If he could find some fruit he was sure it would help. In the morning he would go and look around.

Rurik put some meat on the concave piece of bark which he had scraped on the inside and called to Kito.

"Kito, supper is ready."

Kito opened his eyes and with revulsion looked at the meat in Rurik's extended hand.

"I can't eat. I'm not hungry."

"Kito, you'll have to eat. Come. It isn't so bad." Rurik said caringly.

"I am not hungry."

"Have just a little bit. I also don't feel like eating but we need to eat. Come."

Reluctantly, Kito took the food, holding it as if it were poison. Rurik had to insist that he eat, before he himself took a piece of meat and put it in his mouth. Aversion clearly showed on Kito's face. They both forced the snake meat down in silence, but after swallowing the first piece Kito put the bark on the ground.

"Dad, I really can't eat. If I try to eat anymore I'm going to vomit."

"I know the food doesn't taste good without salt. Tomorrow I'll try to find some fruit or some other food, but if I am not successful we'll have to eat this meat. We must be thankful for what we have. God has helped us."

"God could have sent us something better," Kito replied petulantly.

"Yes, He could have, but He didn't. Perhaps He didn't know you wouldn't like python."

"Isn't God supposed to know everything?" Kito argued.

"Yes, I believe so, but he has also made the law which said you should eat what you are able to provide."

Kito was thoughtful for a moment. "How do you know there is a God? Nobody has seen him," he asked.

For the first time Rurik was glad he had attended church in his youth. When he was Kito's age Rurik had also asked the same question and one Sunday in the church he had gotten an answer.

It was a cold autumn Sunday and a biting northern wind was blowing. Everybody sat in the big church with the stone floor and shivered. Father Spiro was in a particularly foul mood as his voice boomed from the altar. He was obviously displeased with his parishioners, and Rurik suspected it was because they had been slow in bringing the traditional share of their crop into the cellars of the parish house. There had been a bad drought that summer and the crops were poor. Rurik recalled his father arguing with his grandmother during supper, over the quantity of wheat, corn, meat and wine he would take to Father Spiro. Rurik's father maintained that he had to feed the family and that even what he was proposing to take was too much, because the priest, fat as he was couldn't eat or drink all the village's contributions. Rurik's grandmother had been appalled by the language his father had used about a man of God, and crying she went to bed without finishing her supper. The next evening they compromised.

That Sunday Father Spiro lamented about all the villagers being sinners and how they would all go to hell if they didn't mend their ways. He told them how they would be blown away with the ill wind of their own making, like the leaves being blown away by the Bura which howled outside. They would be replaced by a new generation, as the old leaves are every spring. The congregation shivered.

"You can see God if you look." Rurik said. "The wind blows the dead leaves off the trees; they fertilize the soil and give space to new leaves to grow. The water vapor which rises from the sea, rivers and lakes come down in the form of rain to make the seeds grow. One animal eats another in the natural selection of the fittest. We die so new generations will have space. There are endless other examples of His presence. He has created life, time and change. All this is governed by the immutable laws of nature."

"But how do you know God created these laws?" asked Kito.

"You have asked me many questions, as you should. I am here to answer all the questions I can, so you can have the benefit of my knowledge and experience. From there you can advance and hopefully teach your children the truths I have not comprehended in my lifetime. You can even learn from my mistakes. I hope you learn because you have to take the world away from the edge of the abyss to which it has been brought. But don't blame my generation or any previous generation for what was done. That will just waste your time and your generation cannot afford to waste time on recriminations. If you do the world might just go over the precipice.

Now I'll ask you a question. It is obvious that there are all these laws by which every minutest particle in the universe is governed. Who created these laws?"

Perplexed by the change of direction in the conversation Kito looked at Rurik almost accusingly. He opened his mouth to say something, changed his mind and stopped. Rurik looked at him sternly, wanting him to learn not to dismiss something before he had thought it through and had an alternative.

"I don't know... but the laws could have been there." Kito was very uncertain.

"How, if nobody had made them? The laws are perfect, work in harmony and apply throughout the universe. Life comes in myriad shapes and forms and each one has its own cycle and identity. Each one reproduces and adapts, each relates to others and each has thousands or millions of attributes. Generations of people have studied the ant, and still we only have rudimentary knowledge about it. But still, in their arrogance, many deny God, offering one dimensional explanations for the universe. Do not follow that path. It leads to damnation. Earth is just an infinitesimal part of the universe. There must be billions of worlds in the universe and millions of species on each world that I am sure are as complex as life on Earth. All of this is governed by the same law."

"Then God is the law!"

Speechless, Rurik stared at his son in disbelief. Kito had just given him an answer to the question that he had thought was impossible to answer. He had always thirsted for an answer: How did man relate to God? How did man communicate with God? And now his son, a child, had given him the answer.

Kito saw the amazement on Rurik's face and was surprised. He asked, "What's wrong, Dad?"

"Kito, I am astounded. You have just given me an answer to the question I have been asking myself ever since I started thinking about God, and that was when I was about your age."

"That was a long time ago," Kito laughed.

"Yes, it was a long time ago, but now I think I understand man's relationship with God. I think you are right, God is the law and God demonstrates Himself through the law. We keep talking about the law of nature that governs all life. That is the manifestation of God. The more we understand and follow natural laws the closer to God we become and the fuller the life we live."

Rurik's eyes shone with excitement as he spoke. He got up, walked to his son and kissed him on the forehead. "Thank you. You are a clever boy and your mind works well," he said.

Kito smiled shyly and then asked, "But, how do we know what are the laws we must follow?"

"You know what is right and what is wrong. Do not do wrong."

"What if we are not sure?"

"You have to make decisions based on right principles."

"Which are the right principles?"

"You learn those by observing nature. Your mother and I have taught you many, but you always need to learn more. There are many good principles in the books of faith. In spite of different interpretations the principles remain the same. There is only one truth. Different interpretations are refinements to keep functionaries of various religions in business; similar to borders being there to keep various government bureaucracies in business. Imagine the united world where the millions of unemployed politicians, church functionaries and generals who have no other skills but those of manipulation and killing, scramble to divide the world and get back in business."

"You cannot resist criticizing institutions."

"I think you are right there. These people have created many hardships in my life and in millions of other lives. Also these are the people with which your generation will have to deal. Do not underestimate the ability of these people to manipulate the truth."

"Can we always know what is the truth?" Kito asked.

"No, my son, we cannot always know. Otherwise we would be perfect. We would be gods. We will always sin but God will forgive us if we don't understand and punish us if we don't learn. By learning we will come closer to God and our sin will be less."

"So we have to learn?" concluded Kito.

"Yes, we have to learn to follow the law."

"Why didn't you tell me this before?"

"I didn't know."

"How come you know it now?" Kito asked, surprised.

"I have learned."

"How?"

"You asked me questions and I had to think about them. Remember the story I told you about going into the jungle to escape the monotony of everyday life?"

"Yes."

"Well, that's what I did. Your questions have stimulated my thinking, and our predicament has made me see the world from another perspective, making my thinking more lateral."

"I thought you said you had changed your way of thinking when you moved to Black Rock?"

"Yes, I guess I did, but ways of thinking change continually as you learn. Remember a mind that doesn't change is like stale water. Moving to Black Rock was an escape from a confused society directed by social crap instead of natural laws. The other motivation was that I fell in love with your mother. For me it was the perfect combination and I exchanged a world of discontent for a world of bliss."

"What is 'social crap'?"

Rurik laughed. "Social crap is an expression you won't find in literature or the dictionary. In society there are trend setters whom other people follow mindlessly in order to be part of the social scene. There is fierce competition between trend setters to come up with ideas which are different from established norms. Often these ideas are outrageous and different just for the sake of being different. Their only purpose is keeping the trend setter in the public eye. For instance in Hollywood they say that bad publicity is better than no publicity. Throughout decades or maybe even centuries, mindless masses have followed the latest trends causing the moral fibre of society to deteriorate to the point where people have lost direction. Traditional values are negated but nobody can offer a credible alternative. Trend setters are experimenting and people are bewildered." Rurik's voice rose as he spoke.

"At Black Rock the only trend setter was nature with its timeless trend. In addition I only had to pay taxes to the shark that sometimes stole fish from my buoy when I was spearfishing. That I didn't mind so much. I was fishing in the shark's domain and he stole less than ten percent. I think he took my fish only on a bad day, otherwise he caught his own food. And another thing, I must say, the shark was very efficient. I would feel the pull of the line on my weightbelt and I knew the fish was gone. He didn't send any letters or accounts. Remember, you also paid tax once." Rurik teased.

"Yes, I'll never forget. I got such a fright when I felt the pull on my line and then saw the shark getting away with my fish. When I told Mom she was so cross with you and said you shouldn't let me spearfish because I was too small. She thought I should wait on the catamaran."

"Yes, then we cheated and she caught us, but after a while she gave up. Your mom loved you so much and was always afraid for you, but she was very proud when you brought fish. She called you her fisherman."

For a few moments both of them looked into the distance reliving happy days, and then Kito said, "You promised you were going to tell me about you and mom."

"Yes, I did."

Rurik took a stick, pushed burning pieces of wood into the fire and looked into the flames. Kito waited expectantly. A picture of Sandy running down the path and the sun sinking behind the horizon, recreated itself in Rurik's mind, and like a film, their happy times unfolded in his memory.

"Are you going to tell me?" asked Kito impatiently.

"Yes. When I walked back from escorting your mother to the research station I decided to stay for another two days. My food was almost finished and I had to go back to work. The project my agency had was from one of the bigger clients and I didn't want to lose that account. I stayed for another two weeks."

"What about the project you had to do?" Kito asked admiringly.

"I'll come to that. The next day I swam to the reef at high tide but came back without any fish. The following day I went out at low tide and we had fish for supper. What I learned in those two weeks was that I was much happier living in the bay, where I only needed a speargun for my existence, than I was working in Johannesburg. It dawned on me that I had been wasting my life working for things that were superfluous, and what was worse, through my work I had influenced other people to do the same. That was the radical change in my thinking, my first venture into the jungle.

Before I left Black Rock we sat at the edge of the plateau, sparingly sipping the last bottle of wine I had saved. The almost full moon was bathing the bay in a silver light. I was happy. I had a beautiful woman at my side, a speargun in the tent and had demonstrated my ability as a fisherman. I was self-sufficient," Rurik said proudly.

"I had never had more, I realized, but I also knew that in a few days I would be back in my business and then I would again be persuading people that a particular washing powder would make whites whiter, because it had certain enzymes, or it would make washing softer, because it didn't have something else, which neither I nor the people that bought the powder understood. The futility of my occupation was by then crystal clear to me, and I was looking at the surf when your mother asked me if we could stay at Black Rock.

I told her that moonlight was conducive to dreaming and that I had a business to run as well as other responsibilities. I thought she was still young and naive and had never experienced the battle of getting to the top and staying there. She couldn't begin to appreciate the battles I had fought to achieve success and I couldn't seriously consider abandoning what I had worked so long and hard to build.

She said that my responsibility lay in being happy, and that I was happy there and so was she. The moonlight was reflecting off her perfect teeth, giving her playful smile a softness which contrasted with the intensity of her eyes.

I philosophized that happiness was a state of mind and that it comes from within and not from outside. Those days Sandy and I did lots of silly talk because we were young and happy and explored each others' minds. Remember, love is a journey of discovery.

She told me that I was horrible and that I must be nice. I argued that if I was always nice I would be predictable and she would get bored with me and wouldn't love me anymore, because she was an illogical woman. Kito, this I said as a joke but I still think that the predictable bit is true. A woman loses interest if she can predict your reactions. I think you would do well to remember this.

She got cross about the illogical touch. She was confused about what liberated woman are supposed to be like and some of the notions she picked up at university were conflicting with the basics of her upbringing. I often teased her about woman's lib and she called me a male chauvinist pig. I told her I was proud of it, that it was my only chance to retain my identity in a world of woman's lib and how she should hang onto me because she was not likely to find such a rarity again. I also asked if it wasn't chauvinism that we guys were called male chauvinist pigs and woman's libbers were not called female chauvinist sows. I made a point of pressing her on that issue because I was seriously considering marrying your mom, even after the short time we had been together. I had never had similar feelings towards any other girl. I wanted to marry a woman of free spirit, but I wasn't going to marry a woman that was infatuated by social crap. I wanted a mother that would bring my child up and care for it above anything else. Woman's lib was rampant at the time, and the traditional family was being destroyed. The children were caught in the battle of the sexes. Being a mother was seen as a demeaning role. Nobody stopped to think that the noblest and most important job was bringing up new generations. It is a job that is often left to unconcerned institutions or streets if both parents are working.

She was getting really cross and I laughed, kissed her, told her I loved her and we talked late into the night. In the morning we stood on the top of the dune next to the packed fourwheel drive, having our second cup of coffee in silence. The freshness of the ocean floated up to us on the still air.

Sandy interrupted the silence and asked me to come back because we were so happy there. Her sad but eager eyes made me recognize the truth. I didn't want to go. That moment I made a decision.

'I will come back,' I said.

'Permanently?' she asked.

'Permanently,' I said.

She was ecstatic but I had mixed feelings, on the one hand I was happy with my decision and on the other, worried about it.

When I got back to Johannesburg I agonized about my decision and looked for an easy way out. Every weekend I drove to the bay. It took ten hours to get to Black Rock and I drove there on Friday night and back again on Sunday night. The long night drives gave me time for soul searching. One question played on my mind continuously. What if the happiness I was experiencing was just a temporary illusion, and what if the illusion ended and the bay ceased to be a place of bliss? What if I had to come back to advertising again? I had invested much time and energy building my business and didn't cherish the thought of going through the experience again. Eventually I made peace with my decision concluding that I could only live in one world at a time. I sold everything and invested the proceeds.

All my friends and business associates thought I had become a crazy dreamer, influenced by a beautiful woman. You see Kito, people try to keep you back with their gossip. They try to embarrass you so you won't take the step forward. If you do and you are successful it shows them up and makes them feel inferior. It exposes their lack of courage, when compared with yours. If you succeed, they say you were lucky. Gossip is like invisible threads which hold you back.

My decision though, had more strength than those invisible threads and Sandy came to Johannesburg for a few weeks. We got married and shopped for the equipment we needed to be self-sufficient. We bought a bigger tent and a catamaran.

When we left Johannesburg we looked like gypsies. The back of the landrover, roof rack and catamaran were full. It took us two days to get to the bay because in many places we had to hack away growth from the side of the track, so the catamaran could pass. We got to Black Rock exhausted but enthusiastic about our future. We established our camp and in the days that followed we learned how to sail in the light morning wind and generally enjoyed our honeymoon. Well, that is the story. You were born nine months later." With a twinkle in his eye, Rurik watched for Kito's reaction, but Kito, engrossed in the story didn't show any sign of amusement. "Now you need to go to sleep and rest. Tomorrow I'll try to find some fruit and you'll be on your own, so you have to be strong. Take two tablets."

"Tell me more." Kito liked to hear stories, especially one so close to his heart.

"No Kito. We both need rest." Rurik was firm.

Although he was tired, Rurik didn't feel like going to sleep. He decided to sharpen the knife and moved out of the enclosure, so that he wouldn't disturb Kito's sleep. The starlight was bright enough to see the blade. The metallic noise of the stone going over the blade was relaxing and Rurik's mind took him back to the starry night in the bay when he and Sandy had watched the same brilliant stars and decided to name their son Kito. It was the same peaceful night when Sandy and Rurik, inspired by stars that looked like jewels, had decided that Kito was an appropriate name for the boy because it meant jewel and precious child in Swahili.

Rurik pulled the knife over his thumb nail, checking its sharpness. It cut. The sharp pain reminded Rurik that that world belonged to another time. His step was heavy as he walked into the enclosure and pulled the thorny branch behind him. Kito was sleeping, his breathing regular. Rurik thanked God and went to sleep.

In the morning Kito was able to walk. During breakfast Rurik kept cautioning him about safety but he felt a little easier about leaving him alone now that Kito was mobile.

Still, Rurik's repeated warnings prompted Kito to ask anxiously: "You will come back, won't you?"

"Yes, but I could be delayed. If you feel the fever coming back again take the remaining anti malaria tablets. Just make sure the enclosure is always closed."

"You've told me that already," Kito said. Rurik's worry was starting to reflect on Kito and reluctantly Rurik stopped with his advice. He hugged Kito and said good bye. Rurik looked at him through the opening in the enclosure. He was hesitant to leave his son alone and his eyes moistened.

"You are a fighter, Kito," he said and walked down the animal path to the clearing.

The buffalo were not there anymore. A troop of warthog were walking across it, the big male first, followed by the female. Only the tips of the tails of the three piglets were visible, waving above the grass behind the adults. They were too far away for Rurik to attempt to hunt and they disappeared in the bush.

He walked along the edge of the forest looking for fruit, but had no success. He would have to enter the jungle. Fear made him hesitant but he walked on, looking for a passage. He orientated himself by looking at the baobab tree. It towered like a giant above the surrounding forest, its enormous trunk guarding the path to their camp. Rurik tugged at the branches and found an opening. Before he entered he looked back at the baobab tree wishing he could ask the millenniums old giant to guard his son.

Rurik walked for hours, but didn't find any fruit. The sun was overhead already. He was hot and thirsty and a long way from camp. He couldn't decide whether or not to turn back. He sat down and rested his head on his knees. What was the right decision? Go on or go back?

Rurik, sitting lost in thought, was distracted by the annoyingly persistent singing of a bird. Then he realized that the singing sounded familiar. He lifted his head and looked. It was a honey guide.

Legend has it that the honey guide takes man or badger to honey and if they don't leave her her share, the next time she takes them to a black mamba and certain death.

Rurik wondered if somebody like him had passed here before and had not left her her fair share. Another man? Rurik needed the honey; his son's life might depend on it. He would leave her her fair share. Rurik followed the bird. He tried to memorize the direction in which he was walking but became more and more confused.

Then Rurik heard the buzzing of bees and then one flew through the beam of light that the sun cast through the branches onto the jungle floor, and then another. As he moved forward more and more bees were caught in the beams, building a very dangerous wall in Rurik's path. Then he saw that the bees were coming from a Y-shaped hole in the tree and knew he had found honey.

He made a fire and the green branches gave off clouds of smoke. The smoke enraged the bees and they flew around furiously. Rurik moved away fast. He found a wild banana tree and cut it down to use as material for a container. He gauged out the soft inside, made two holes at the top, opposite each other, put the hard creeper through the holes and tied them onto two sticks on the inside.

The bird complained loudly. All she had received for her effort was foul air. Rurik's nerves were raw, the noise screeched discordantly in his ears and he wished that she would shut up.

Dead bees were lying around the fire, burnt or smoked to death. Rurik pulled the bees' nursery out piece by piece, and put the honey onto the banana leaves. It glittered, its intricate and symmetrical form reflecting the sunbeams in all directions. The bird was quiet now, probably because she had seen the honey.

Rurik divided the honey into three parts, two for Kito and himself and the third for the bird. The builders of the Okavango islands, the ants, claimed their share too. Rurik put his and Kito's share into the container and licked his fingers until the taste buds on his tongue couldn't detect the delicious sweetness anymore.

He walked in the direction from which he had come, orientating himself by the sun and hoping he would find the way back to Kito. Rurik thought he recognized some of the trees and felt growing excitement at being with his son again and being able to give him the honey.

After a while Rurik realized he shouldn't have eaten the honey. He was really thirsty now. The thirst drove him forward, overwhelming every other sensation. Fatigue, worry and scratches from the thorns and branches were of no concern anymore. Relentlessly, he moved on. The beams of light streamed through the branches at ever increasing angles and Rurik began to panic.

Suddenly there were no beams anymore. He had emerged into a bright, sunlit clearing and there was water. He ran toward it, took the container off his back and kneeled to drink. He drank a little, fighting his urge, knowing he could get ill if he drank too much at one time. Then drank some more, many times.

Rurik stood up and looked around. What a clearing this was! As far as the eye could reach, interspersed by termite islands with palm trees, it stretched into eternity. In groups or singly animals grazed, the far ones just dark spots on the landscape. Buffalo, zebra, giraffe, springbok, wildebeest and elephant intermingled on the plain in numbers that amazed Rurik. He saw a cheetah, followed by three cubs walk towards a group of springbok. The springbok grazed, keeping a safe distance, while the nearby buffalo paid no attention to the cheetah. The late afternoon sun reflected off the water. Beyond the water he saw the outline of the forest which curved far south and joined the wall of trees from which he had come. Awed by the space and the abundance of animals, he imagined that this was what the first adventurers had found when they came to Africa.

Then Rurik saw the baobab tree. It towered above the rest, less impressive than he remembered, because of the distance, no doubt.

Elated, Rurik hurried and animals moved from his path. It was a long but easy walk. The prospect of being together with his son urged him forward. Before he entered the forest he looked back to once more see this incredible plain which the setting sun bathed in the mellow light of tranquillity.

He entered the forest and lost sight of the baobab tree, but remembered the direction. Even if he lost direction some, the clearing was big enough and he couldn't miss it. Sunlight was touching the tops of the tall trees when he saw the clearing. The wrong clearing! The baobab was growing in the middle of it.

Rurik dashed back in panic. He had to get back to the water before it got dark. From there he had to try and figure out the way back to Kito. He realized the enormity of the risk he had taken and castigated himself. What had he done? He had left Kito alone. He had abandoned his son! Tears of frustration rolled from his eyes. As he ran out of the forest he saw the sun about to sink into the horizon, reflecting like a burning spear off the distant water. Rurik ran.

The hooves of the animals had made countless indentations on the ground. The sun had set. Rurik ran faster. He stumbled frequently but kept running. The honey ran stickily down his back. He imagined Kito lying helpless in the enclosure.

Rurik's foot caught and he fell. The last thing he saw was a small termite mound, a future island. He hit it with the side of his head and the dusk became impenetrable night.

8

Madala listened to the male pygmy duck, the prettiest of the Okavango waterfowl, whistle softly to its mate as he poled his mokoro with a vigor he had not experienced since the days of his youth. His senses were freed from the indifference of aimlessness and he appreciated the profusion of life around him. A kingfisher hovered above the water for a moment before diving with deadly accuracy to catch a fish, and an African Jacana bird supported by its enormous splayed feet, walked on the floating vegetation, while its nest of four yellow eggs, criss-crossed by black lines, lay camouflaged on a lily leaf. A pair of dragonflies flew coupled together in an act of love and recreation. Madala drove through spider webs suspended between papyrus stalks, deadly barricades for flying insects, and admired the beauty of the brown male eagle sitting on a perch high above the swamp. Madala's approach scared white egrets searching for fish, tadpoles and insects in the shallows of the swamp. As they flew away he followed their flight into the blue cloudless sky until they descended to continue their search for sustenance.

This was the second day of his journey back, initiated by the death of the Sitatunga. Still, Madala had no idea of how to counter the powerful forces of destruction. At least he was certain of one thing, humans were the species in whose hands the fate of others rested. The only solution, making man accept that he had to change his ways, totally occupied Madala's thinking.

Despite his new-found vigor, he knew that time was short for the mission he had set for himself. He had to rest again today in spite of the urgency to find Dr.Adams. He could no longer pole the mokoro day and night in the blazing sun or rain, as he could when he was younger.

The weather was going to change and there was a good chance of a storm within the next few days. Madala chose an island where he would spend the night and pointed the mokoro in its direction. As he moored his dugout the sun sank behind the forest. He would have to bail water again in the morning before he left.

Madala made a fire with his firesticks and roasted a few mopani worms. He sat chewing the nutritious worms as the flames warmed his wrinkled body. He wondered whether it was the Spirit that had turned him back or his own tormented mind desperate for peace and forgiveness. Would he achieve his objective with this, his last journey of purpose? Doubt always seemed to come at night when he was tired and unoccupied with any activity.

He had no option but to go back, he thought. Staying in the swamp served no purpose. He had wasted the last seven years by mourning a world which wasn't dead yet. It was a flight from reality which he had not stayed to confront *because* he had believed that he was inadequate. Now, reality that the animal world was vanishing under the onslaught of humankind was haunting him day and night. Dr.Adams was right. He had stayed to fight. The compromises of conferences were victories and not defeats. Before the conferences there had been no compromises.

Madala added a few pieces of wood to the fire. No longer warm, he felt as though the moist air was draining his energy which his own retreating life-force wasn't able to replenish.

He would never give up again. It was the only way to succeed.

Madala thought about the tortoise and the Sitatunga and wondered why the death of the Sitatunga had touched so deeply someone who had killed throughout his life. Perhaps it was the tortoise and not the Sitatunga that had revealed The Spirit to him by showing him its total dependence on his will. It had just taken time for him to realize the absolute power man had over the life or death of an animal. Of course it took time. His instinct of self-justification would have fought hard against the acceptance of the burdening truth. On the other hand it could have been his loneliness and self-examination which inspired him to reach The Spirit. The tortoise and Sitatunga were just the final pieces in the puzzle. Doubt was hard at work, but Madala fought.

He gazed at the burning branch and considered the cyclical nature of life and death. His mind followed the dead branch back to the tree, green with leaves and seeds. He imagined the tree when it was a young shoot, and then when it was a seed. He pictured the dead branch dropping the seed before it had died and with sudden clarity Madala grasped that the branch hadn't died. It had just became young again, just changed the body. He could do it too. Implant his spirit in a young body and let the old one go. The old one was giving him trouble anyhow. He had ample time to achieve his ultimate objective Madala thought exhilarated. All he had to do was find a young body.

Madala felt peace, only attained by the man who has perceived that he is being guided by divine force. It was past midnight as the old man watched a red moon rise and give the swamp an ethereal and illusory look. By the time the moon was overhead the basis of a plan had formed in Madala's head. Content in the belief that he was a step closer to a solution and that tomorrow he would be further along the path, he went to sleep.

Madala woke with the first light and ate the yellow, sweet berries he found on the Motsoadi tree nearby. He bailed the water out of the mokoro and pointed his craft south, his mind occupied with the revelations of the previous night.

The only solution, Madala reasoned, was to find a younger man with sound basic values, onto whom he could pass his experience and the belief that the well-being of all mankind was dependant on the success of conservation. That would extend his time by decades or even in perpetuity. The rhino or cheetah didn't have decades, but maybe the elephant and the lion did.

He hoped Dr.Adams had a young, bright and enthusiastic assistant. But what if Dr.Adams was dead and his work forgotten? Madala reprimanded himself. Seven years of negative thinking was enough and hadn't led to a solution. He had to work on his approach.

Whoever he found would need to be convinced of the rightness and viability of Madala's goal. He knew he would encounter arguments. Dr.Adams always had, and Madala knew what they would be. The first and the most difficult to counter would be, that one couldn't subordinate peoples' rights to animal rights. Yes we care about the animals and the environment, the argument would go, but what about the needs of people? *You cannot stop progress!*

Madala considered his reply. He could say that every day there were more people, each with more needs, but that every day there were fewer animals and trees whose needs never changed. They only needed the space given to them. Man had no right to take it away. Why couldn't space be shared in a responsible manner? The next argument would be that every man had the right to prosperity and that natural resources had to be used for the benefit of mankind.

Mankind's needs are perverted and resources are used inefficiently and wastefully, and if there are not enough resources mankind should limit its numbers, he would say.

Madala knew that he would be accused of insensitivity towards the poor and deprived, who multiplied the fastest due to lack of education. He would be labelled a lunatic. Madala couldn't allow that to happen; then nobody would listen to him. He had to find better arguments if he was to succeed.

The old man poled while the sun rose and he analyzed human thinking. He failed to understand why man would want two mokoros. One gave him freedom of movement, while the other held him back. This was sin of the rich. They acquired things they seldom used, creating a need in others to whom they had become symbols of success. Madala knew that he would get endless arguments about different people and varied needs, so he would also have to be careful about pushing the values which had ensured the abundance of wildlife throughout Africa. His people had been called savages by the race to which he had to appeal, and nobody adopted values of savages. He would have to be careful. Not all of his people's actions were right. There was good in white people too. The problem was that people justified their bad deeds with the bad deeds of others.

Madala struggled to define values which everybody could embrace and which would enable man to accept that God had created animal, tree and man, and had given them equal right to space and life. Madala poled and the sun rose. He explored various options of approach but then argued them from the perspective of current social philosophy. When the sun became too hot he moored at an island to rest and gather some food.

It was pleasant walking through the bush with branches blocking the blazing sun, and soon he heard baboons feeding. Madala walked in the direction of the sound knowing that he would find fruit, when he heard the grunt of a baby hippo. His body straightened a little and his step became more cautious. Where there was a baby, there was always the danger of the protective mother.

A few more careful steps and he spotted monkeys on a wild fig, enjoying the ripe fruit. Madala heard another grunt beyond the wild fig and cautiously approached, but he couldn't see the source. Before he picked any figs he had to see where the hippo was, so he didn't find himself in a dangerous position.

As he approached the water he saw eight stonelike shapes lying motionless in the mud of the lagoon. The ninth, a smaller one, grunted and rolled in the shallow water. A group of crocodiles were sunning on the mudbank behind the hippo, while one walked along the water's edge, its huge tail trailing behind. The little hippo didn't pay any attention to the approaching crocodile and continued to enjoy the muddy water, to the annoyance of the adults who grunted angrily every time the youngster bumped into them.

Stealthily the crocodile closed the gap and then stopped a few meters away. Its body blended with the mud. He waited for the unsuspecting prey to come within the reach of its jaw. Madala watched this game of life, fascinated by the sudden realization that the crocodile had probably played the same game with the young of the dinosaurs.

The baby hippo ignored the threat and played closer to the reptile, challenging the waiting predator. The crocodile lunged forward, its jaws wide open. The youngster grunted in fear, pivoted his bulky body on his hind legs, narrowly avoiding the jaw about to close around his neck. The crocodile regained its momentum as its front legs touched the mud and slithered after the retreating hippo, whose desperate grunts had excited the adults.

As the baby moved between two adults the crocodile lunged again and missed. Now the crocodile and baby hippo were in-between the adults and huge jaws snapped at the reptile, the hunter now the hunted. Unable to turn back, the crocodile jumped on the baby's back and from there onto the back of the nearest adult. Jaws snapped, narrowly missing the reptile which sprinted from one massive back onto the other, jumped off the last hippo and hurriedly slithered a safe distance away. The hippo grunted for a while and then settled back into their midday rest with the baby in-between the adults.

Madala was just about to climb the fig tree when the crocodile moved closer to the hippo again. It lay at almost the same place it had waited before. Nothing moved, and had Madala not witnessed the attack, the peaceful scene would have deceived even him. He waited while the baboons above him continued to feed, totally unperturbed by the drama in the mud. Again, the baby hippo pushed his way out of the protective shield.

This time the crocodile didn't wait long and as soon as the hippo had wandered a few steps from the adults he quickly attacked, but not quickly enough to avoid the cavernous jaw and arm-thick teeth of the nearest adult hippo. The crunching sound signified the breaking of the crocodile's spine. The hippo swung its head, shaking the broken, twitching body and threw it away, and now the broken body, tail still twitching, lay in the mud. Madala, amused by the folly of the attack, watched until the tail stopped twitching and peace returned to the swamp. Even the baby hippo settled between the adults to await the feeding time of the late afternoon.

The chatter of the baboons above reminded Madala about the figs. He climbed onto the lower branch paying no attention to the monkeys. While he ate he kept an eye on the swamp. The picture of absolute peace stayed unchanged, everybody contented at the elimination of the disturbance. When he had had enough to eat, Madala climbed down and threw a last glance at the peaceful scene before he walked back to his mokoro to rest.

He lay against the tree with his eyes closed, a picture of the peaceful aftermath of the battle in his mind as he slipped into a relaxing sleep. When he awoke the picture was still there and nagged at him throughout the afternoon. The scene lurked in the deep recesses of his mind waiting for an opportunity to slip forward and Madala couldn't concentrate. His mind jumped from one argument he was going to put forward to another.

A dark shadow clouded his soul as he boiled the stew of lily bulbs that evening. Madala sat against the trunk and watched the stars which had given him direction throughout his life. The stars were something that never changed. They were always at the same place at the same time of the year. They all had their place in time. Perhaps he was like one of the stars, in his place in his time. If something guided billions of stars along their paths, then that something must be guiding him along his path. He must be doing what he was destined to do! The thought transformed Madala. The dark shadow dissipated and peace lightened his senses. The contrasting sensations, created by a burdened spirit and an easy mind, gave birth to the answer he had been so desperately seeking.

Peace of mind was the value everybody would embrace. That was his base, he thought excitedly. Nobody could argue about the benefit of peace.

Now Madala contemplated how to unify the concept of peace with his objective. He looked at the stars again. Orion had moved further west. It had no choice but to follow the path it had always followed, but Madala could travel in any direction he chose. A free mind was a problem at times.

Madala recalled the picture of the crocodile and hippo, and he suddenly understood why the scene kept returning to his mind so persistently. It was the peace after the elimination of the disturbance that was the key to the resolution of his problem, but his confused mind hadn't been able to perceive it. His unhappiness and subsequent relief had made him see the difference between the heaviness and lightness of the mind. That resulted in the recognition that all people carry burdens, and those burdens prevent them from achieving peace of mind.

The majority try to attain this by creating wealth, but the problem with wealth is that there is always a need for more, but less and less is available. Then paper wealth is created, an illusion. That increases the insecurity and the worry about the future. The burden becomes heavier, and the fight for resources becomes fiercer. The fears about the future were justified. He had seen how finite the seemingly unlimited wildlife of the Okavango was. Man would run out of resources, not only material but also spiritual, because he would be alone.

Madala understood this well; he saw death of epic proportions. Surely that was the sign of major readjustment in the world. Life had become so expendable and nobody cared. The human race had become callous, it had lost its soul. Why was this occurring now, in his lifetime, he wondered. Yes, why in his lifetime? His was just one of countless generations, which had gone and which could come. It could have happened later or earlier so he wouldn't have known the beauty of this world, and its impending demise would not weigh on his conscience. He tried to imagine a world with no animals and no trees and he saw a desert where nothing could live, more barren than the sands of the Kalahari.

The moon had risen, diminishing the light of the stars, casting an ethereal glow over the swamp. The change was happening during his life as a challenge to him. The enormity of this task overwhelmed Madala, but his mind plodded on. He needed to find another man and, united with a common destiny, they had to ensure that there was a future, and hope for a new generation. They had to find a way to change the direction. For the first time Madala appreciated the full significance of Dr. Adams's work. He felt guilt at having left him to fight alone. Madala hoped that Dr. Adams was still alive so that he could tell him how much he respected him for his courage, and how much time he had given to others to find a solution.

Madala couldn't sleep and the moon was already above the tree where he couldn't see it, but he did see the silver light illuminating his universe. It was imperative to make people see that epic changes are a challenge to them, and then surely, they would understand the urgent need for a change of morality. The moonlight was already giving way to the brilliance of the stars before Madala fell asleep, but he was up before sunrise, eagerly poling his mokoro. He poled through the heat of the day, only stopping to bail out water and eat a few mopani worms, hoping that with every push of the pole he was closer to Dr. Adams.

His old body ached under the strain and hurt from the effort, but Madala forced his body to pole until the sun touched the horizon. He succumbed to fatigue and slept, exhausted, but happy in the knowledge that he had won over the weakness of the body and that tomorrow he would win again. The next morning Madala drove through the swamp that had changed from permanent to perennial. Occasionally he travelled past the plains, observing the abundance of life which inhabited this vastness interspersed by thousands of unnamed islands. It was as if nature was guiding him through this animal paradise to show off her bounty. He pushed the pole with vigor that only a determined mind could extract from an old body.

Driving past another plain he saw an elephant, a solitary bull in his prime that dwarfed every other animal on the plain. There were not many elephants left in the Okavango. When he had left Dr.Adams, only two thousand remained where tens of thousands used to roam before.

The tusks of the great bull nearly touched the ground, Madala noticed that they matched in size, except that one bent inwards. He watched the elephant walk across the plain towards the distant forest. Soon he was hidden by one of the palm islands and Madala wondered about the elephant's destiny.

As he raised his eyes, Madala saw a column of smoke rising into the air far ahead beyond the forest. The sign of another man. He felt a sense of excitement coupled with doubt. For seven years he had not communicated with another human being. Today, before the sun reached its zenith, he would begin a relationship which would be different from any other. Now Madala understood that his mission and the mission of the other man was the same. He hoped that the other man understood it too. What if he didn't? One thing at a time, Madala thought. First meet the man. He pushed the pole into the water, speeding the mokoro towards the encounter.

9

Rurik woke with a headache. He sat up and looked around, thinking he must be dreaming. What a paradise! The cloudless sky, bonded to the earth by a fine mist had a mystical soft blue glow. Animals grazed on the endless plain, far ones dots in the distance. Zebras, wildebeest and springbok mingled in a rough circle around him. A herd of a few hundred buffalo grazed between Rurik and the forest. A solitary elephant, with one tusk bent inwards, dominated the plain.

A few meters away an axe was lying, a spear just beyond it. He felt the bump on his temple and the pain dispelled the illusion of a dream. Rurik stood up and staggered. Where was he? He turned, saw a container crawling with ants and felt intuitively that it had some significance. He strained to remember but in his mind there was a vast empty space surrounded by mist.

A vague memory nagged at the edge of his consciousness. He struggled to capture the elusive picture. Through the mist, he saw his childhood home. He tried to bring the picture into focus but the vision shimmered, ethereal, just out of reach. Rocky hills with hardy shrubs were vague, and the picture of his parents danced elusively in the mist. Still, he felt child-like security in the memory. A sense of love filled his soul and with it the face of a boy came to his mind. The rising sun evaporated the mist and the vague and comforting picture of home and his parents began to dissolve. Rurik's security evaporated. What had happened since he had left his home and who was the boy? It was all so unreal and confusing. He was an adult, but he couldn't remember his adulthood. He felt abandoned and alone and wished his parents were here. On his left was the forest, in front the immense plain with animals and a few hundred meters away the sharp end of the wedge of the water.

Rurik picked up the axe and the spear, uncertain where to go. He sensed that he couldn't stay where he was, but he didn't know where to go. His thirst drew him towards the water. As he got closer he could see palm islands reflected in it, creating an image of two identical worlds. He knelt to drink and saw his bearded face. A bow-shaped scar ran from above his left eye to the cheekbone. Rurik drank, washed his face and stood up, feeling like a lost child.

Again he tried to penetrate the mist of the past, in vain. Where should he go? Where was he? Whose world was this and how did he get here? He stood immobilized by indecision when the elephant captured his attention. The giant pulled up a tuft of long grass with his trunk, swung it through the air and beat it a few times against his leg. Each blow created a cloud of dust which floated away on a gentle breeze. The elephant put the grass into his mouth and chewed stolidly, looking directly at Rurik. He looked content and Rurik wished he felt the same kind of security that the elephant's unconcerned posture projected. Rurik felt that he needed to get closer to the giant, sensing that somehow his own security would be enhanced. Alone he felt so insecure. He walked closer to the elephant, between the water and the buffalo, keeping a respectful distance from the herd.

He entered the tall grass, instinctively careful of hidden dangers. About fifty paces ahead he saw a pair of tawny ears. Rurik froze. Below the ears, camouflaged by the grass, he saw a lion's head, dangerously still. As the breeze swayed the grass he saw another pair of ears, and then another, all of them motionless. The stillness was almost palpable. Some past knowledge told Rurik that the slightest movement on his part would pose a challenge and a threat. Did the lions know he was here? How could he become invisible? He sank slowly, concealing himself in the long grass.

The lions were patient and time seemed to stand still. He could only see the closest one through the grass as he squatted patiently and watched. His knees began to hurt; he had been squatting too long. He sank down on one knee, the other leg ready to lift him fast, then later he changed legs. The sun was still behind him, above the eastern horizon, its rays revealing the peaceful scene. The buffalo were moving closer.

Then the predator moved. It was a lioness. She moved stealthily, staying hidden behind the grass, always watching the buffaloes. Excitement at the anticipation of the hunt overtook Rurik, the lioness was going for the kill. Her posture gave her away. Then another lioness appeared, following the first, then another two.

At first the buffalo seemed unaware of all this activity and then an old bull smelled the wind. The first lioness was upwind already. The bull had smelt the danger. He jumped and started running. Panic-stricken, the herd followed.

Rurik stood up, all thoughts of his own safety forgotten. He saw the lionesses spring into action. The buffalo was going to get away, Rurik thought as he watched the gap between the buffalo and lionesses increase. Then the buffaloes changed direction, all but a young bull in the forefront of the fleeing herd. Right behind him was a lioness, previously hidden in the grass, waiting in ambush. The buffalo tried to run into the forest but it was too late. The distance between the hunter and the hunted diminished fast and the lioness was stretched almost flat in the flight of the chase.

The other four lionesses changed direction and raced to cut off the retreat. The gap between the fifth lioness and the buffalo closed. She was running alongside the buffalo and now a kill was certain. She sprung on his neck and hung there precariously, trying to break the buffalo's spine.

The other lionesses were closing in and the first to reach the buffalo jumped onto his rump and dragged him down while the second tore at his throat. The buffalo gave up the struggle knowing that he had lost. Rurik heard a mournful bellow which filled him with dread.

Within moments the plain was calm and tranquil. The rest of the herd watched the unfolding drama and then started grazing again. The old bull continued to watch, probably wondering when his turn was going to come. He looked around at his herd and then he too started grazing.

Rurik was about to continue his walk when he saw a black maned lion stand up from the grass not far from him. Fear paralyzed him. The lion must have seen Rurik and watched him all the time the hunt was on. Royally, he now walked to the kill and passed Rurik without a second glance.

As the lion approached the kill, he growled at the lionesses who had opened the belly and were eating hungrily. As the male came closer they ate more urgently, then four of them retreated. One was slower or greedier and a mighty paw and roar of the male made her retreat, her posture submissive. The king started eating leisurely. Gradually, the females joined in.

Rurik watched the lions eat, his mouth watering. How could he get a share of the meat? The buffalo was so big he couldn't imagine the lions eating it all. He sat down, watched and waited. There would be something left. How had he obtained food in the past? He tried to see through the mist in his mind, but had no success. There were traces of blood on the sheath of his knife so he must have killed before. He looked at the animals on the plain, but they all kept a safe distance. The elephant was still there, close to the lions. To him the lion wasn't the king. Rurik envied the elephant and, his adulthood blanked from his mind, childishly wished to be like the giant. He wanted to be the elephant's brother.

The calm and majestic elephant looked at him for a long time. His huge ears flapped rhythmically, cooling the massive body. His trunk, perpendicular lines running across it, narrowed from the skull and hung down into the grass. His giant body was commanding but his eyes looked caring. Perhaps the elephant could read his thoughts. Rurik felt more secure, the elephant was stronger than the lion. He was an emperor and perhaps might become his ally. He would stay close to Emperor even if he didn't become Rurik's ally. Emperor's presence might protect him.

It was becoming hot now and Rurik looked at the sun. High above the lions and the kill the vultures were circling, gliding effortlessly on the thermals. Keeping low, so as not to invite unnecessary attention from the lions, he moved into the shade, closer to the elephant. His feeling of security increased.

The lions were eating leisurely. Now Rurik's stomach was grumbling. The vultures had landed and were circling the kill at a safe distance. Some of them took chances and the adventurous ones would run, grab a scrap of intestine and retreat fast, flapping their wings to help them along. Now the black maned lion was rolling on the carcass. The lionesses still ate lazily.

Rurik wished the lionesses were not so gluttonous. He really felt that they should stop eating and go. By now all the vultures were getting their scraps and Rurik had a horrible feeling that they were going to eat it all, and nothing would be left for him. Rurik became convinced that they were all working together to deny him his share of the food. The lions would eat the meat and the vultures would pick the bones clean. From the corner of his eye he noticed another movement. It was a hyaena. It would eat the bones and nothing would be left.

Rage rushed blood into Rurik's head. He wouldn't let them do it. He had to get his share. Irrational anger blinded him. He grabbed the spear with his left hand and looked for something to throw at the lions. He grabbed two pieces of dead wood and ran towards the lions screaming. Startled, the lions stood up and looked at the noisy creature running at them. When he judged he was close enough, Rurik threw one piece of wood. It made the lions move back a little. The male growled and it looked as though he was going to attack. Boiling with childish jealousy, Rurik ran even closer and threw another piece. It flew high, landed on the curved horn of the carcass and ricocheted towards the male. He jumped back. Rurik kept screaming and slowly approached. The lions, their stomachs full, retreated to the water.

Rurik attacked the vultures and some dispersed while the ones behind his back kept grabbing pieces of meat. He continued attacking until his rage subsided. They were not braver than he. He had chased the lions away. He walked to the carcass and cut off a piece of meat still left on the shoulder and looked at the lions. They were drinking water, unconcerned with Rurik. He sunk his teeth into the meat. It tasted good. Blood ran through his beard and he wiped it off with the back of his hand, then he walked back into the shade. Emperor, his posture proud, looked at Rurik. As their eyes met Rurik felt an enormous sense of security. His decision to stay with the elephant was a good one, he thought.

As his hunger subsided, Rurik's stomach started rebelling at the raw meat and he threw the rest away. The lions were lying in the shade of a palm island. The fear of the lions, that Rurik had felt before, was gone. They had retreated. With a feeling of importance, he went to drink water.

For the rest of the afternoon he lay in the shade, relaxing. Life was not that hard after all. If he only knew who he was and where he had come from. The feeling that he had to go somewhere nagged at him as he watched the world around him. Emperor had stopped in the shade of a great tree and stood there for most of the afternoon. The world and time stood still in the oppressive heat.

Rurik considered his experiences of the day. Now that he had food in his stomach, he understood the foolishness of his deed. In future he would have to obtain food in less risky ways. The lions had killed the buffalo, who was after all stronger and faster than him. He recalled how unconcerned the male lion had been when he walked past Rurik. He hadn't even given him a second glance which now that he thought about it offended Rurik's importance. The only difference, he realized, was that when he had chased the lions away, they were not hungry. Now that he too was not hungry, he also thought differently.

Rurik again tried to disentangle his past, but still it remained a mystery. The afternoon moved along and the breeze coming from the west became cooler and stronger. A line of clouds formed on the horizon just below the sun. As Emperor started to eat again he moved westwards and Rurik followed.

Initially the line of clouds seemed tied to the horizon but then they moved fast. Soon the dark wall hid the sun and gradually darkness spread over the plain. The breeze became a strong wind and Rurik's simple and unquestioning contentment developed into fear. Emperor seemed unconcerned but most of the other animals were leaving the plain, heading for the forest. The wind stopped abruptly and the birds ceased singing. Silence fell, broken only by the deep rumble of thunder.

The first drops of rain provoked a very uncomfortable feeling in Rurik. The coming night wouldn't be easy. The entire sky was now black and a sudden gust of wind brought a wall of rain. A last glance in the direction of Emperor revealed only a hint of the shadow which blended with the dark wall of the forest.

Rurik ran for the shadow, terrified that he would lose contact with the only being that gave him security and a sense of closeness. Until now, he had kept a good distance from the elephant because he was scared to come close, but now he was more scared of being separated from Emperor, and being alone.

Please Emperor don't leave me, Rurik thought. Stay with me. You know this, your world. You know where you are, but me, I am lost. I don't even know who I am. The only anchor I have is you. You are the only sanctuary I know aside from the vague picture hidden in the mist of time, but I cannot travel through time. You are the only one in my time with whom I have contact. Please do not leave, stay with me.

The rain and darkness blinded Rurik. His foot hooked onto a piece of dead wood and he staggered, but managed to maintain his balance. He walked slowly now, his hands outstretched, listening for a big body moving through the bush. The wind gusted around his ears, swinging branches which hit his head and body. His hands and ears probed the darkness and at one point Rurik felt as though he was being shielded. He reached into the wind but felt nothing. He took one step to his right and then another. On the second step he hit a rise and bent down to feel it. A steep incline sloped away from him. The wind was not so strong here. He felt for the shape of the slope and sat down. One side felt like a huge leg, sandy and rough. He sat on the inside of it, protected from the wind. Now he felt more secure. Rurik wondered where the elephant was and if he too was secure. The wind was breaking branches and trees. Sharp cracks echoed through the darkness.

Rurik listened to the storm moving east. He was tired and closed his eyes wondering whether he would ever see Emperor again. He was aware that the wind was diminishing and the rain was lessening. Soon the rain stopped and he slept until morning.

The ants in his beard woke Rurik up and he opened his eyes and scratched his beard. He turned around to see what had given him protection and froze in shock.

The movement of his head caused the movement of another head, dark and deadly. The huge dark snake was curled on the ant-hill against which he was sitting. His eyes were a blink away from hers. The reptile's round eyes, with dark pupils, hypnotized Rurik and he stared unmoving at the frightening serpent. The scales on its belly were light in color, changing to light brown on the sides, and from dark brown to black on the back. The mouth ran the entire length of the snake's head. The nostrils, two slits at the front of the head gave it an uncaring, matter-of-fact, demeanor. The snake looked deadly. If it struck it would strike at his head. A three-and-a-half meter reptile, thick as his arm, held him in its power. There was no way out. He stared into the black eyes of death, his senses numbed. Ants crawled through his hair and beard and the impulse to scratch was almost irresistible but he dared not move.

Then Rurik heard a crack in the forest followed by the noise of something moving through the bush, getting louder and louder as it approached. The snake's head tilted slightly. Was it going to strike? The noise of breaking branches was loud now and the snake's head moved again. Rurik wanted to look, but didn't dare. He waited for death.

Then Emperor appeared. Only he could move through the bush so noisily and fearlessly. Rurik shifted his eyes a little, the elephant looked menacing as he walked towards him. The decision of life or death was imminent. Rurik couldn't move away. His movement would provoke the snake. He waited. Emperor kept coming, breaking the branches and stepping on saplings. He was almost upon them when Rurik saw him step onto a long straight sapling that bent under his weight. He closed his eyes expecting a blow. Leaves touched his face and he knew the blow would follow. The trunk crashed onto the anthill and he opened his eyes. The snake was gone.

Emperor kept walking, paying no attention to Rurik. On the inside of the bent tusk there was a gash shaped like a bow, almost the same shape as the scar on Rurik's temple. We are kin! Rurik thought. Emperor walked as if he had an aim and a destination in mind. Rurik followed Emperor most of the morning, but Emperor didn't acknowledge his presence. Rurik was getting annoyed and tired of walking.

My friend, maybe you just accidentally stood on that sapling and now want to take credit, Rurik thought. I can see it in the importance of your walk. Anyway what can a snake do to you? Big deal.

The elephant kept walking until they emerged from the forest, close to the water. They both had a drink and then the elephant fed leisurely. Rurik followed keeping a safe distance. Today everything was calm on the plain. Rurik wasn't sure, but it seemed they were on the same plain on which they had been yesterday, but much further west. Again there was a multitude of animals as far as Rurik could see, and all of them were eating, except Rurik.

Hungry, tired and annoyed that nobody cared about him, not even Emperor who was his hero, Rurik thought he should maybe speak to him. What should he say? He should complain. Hey you, big stuff, he should say, if you are so important, why don't you find me some food? I also need to eat, but I don't eat the stuff you eat. There are plenty of leaves around and they don't run away when you approach. How do I find food? I am a stranger here; it seems. This is your turf, show me how good you are. I need food, find me some. You walk so fast and I am not as big as you are. Be my friend. You must know how I feel. I am hungry.

Emperor stopped at a leafy tree and started to eat. How could an elephant provide him with food, Rurik thought. He looked around, hoping that he could get close to one of the animals which he could kill, but all of them kept a distance. He walked through the forest looking for prey always knowing where Emperor was. He didn't want to get separated from his only friend again. The sound of breaking branches gave away his position. Emperor was so careless. He would break a branch just for convenience or just because it was in front of him or had tastier leaves than the lower branches. He pushed trees down as well, rocking them with his massive head, until they fell, uprooted or broken. He would then feed at leisure.

Then unexpectedly Rurik had his chance to kill. A squirrel stood on a branch within his reach. One swing with the axe would almost certainly kill her. She looked at him inquiringly, as if she wanted to know who he was. He wondered what *she* thought. There was not much meat on her, she was so small. She was a beautiful creature and didn't seem to be afraid of Rurik. He smiled at her.

Emperor's head appeared through the bushes, he looked at Rurik and then turned his head away. He seemed to be cross as he walked into the bush. Rurik looked at the squirrel.

"Did you see? He was jealous. Come with me and we'll give that big bull a hard time. Who does he think he is anyway? But we must follow him. He is not so bad. This morning he even saved my life. I know he did, but I was teasing him about it happening by accident."

The squirrel lifted her head in a quick motion, questioningly.

"Yes, he did. He is just grumpy. Let's go."

The elephant walked fast now, without stopping, and Rurik had difficulty following. Sometimes he would spot a squirrel in the branches and wondered if it was the same one. They walked for a long time. Emperor was really cross, Rurik thought.

What is your problem? he thought. I only smiled at her. Why shouldn't I have another friend. You are just an old grumpy bull. She can be your friend too. We can all be friends. Come on, don't walk so fast. I am getting tired, you know. Have you forgotten that I have had nothing to eat? I've only had a few drinks of water today.

Emperor carried on unconcerned.

Okay, she can be only your friend. It is not fair, but if you want it that way, it's okay. Where is she anyhow? I haven't seen her for a while. You must have chased her away with your grumpiness. She was playful and happy. Who wants to associate with somebody as grumpy as you? Well, I do, but I am an exception, not everybody is like me. You better remember that. Please, slow down. I really am tired.

Emperor just walked on.

Okay, I will show you that I can walk too. You are not such a big deal after all. After a while they entered a clearing and in the centre of it stood a tree full of yellow and green marulas. Many lay on the ground. They looked delicious. Rurik's majestic friend didn't stop to eat. He just walked across the clearing, squashing the fruit.

Rurik bent to pick up a marula, when the tree shook and marulas rained down like projectiles. One hit Rurik on the head, two on his back. It hurt. He pulled back. The tree swung wildly under the onslaught of the mighty head.

"You don't have to do that. You do not have to throw fruit at me. If it's yours, it's yours. You can have it! I don't want any of your food, even if I have to starve."

Rurik rubbed his head as he spoke. He squatted at the edge of the clearing. The elephant came at him. He looked frightening. Rurik had never been this close to him before and he was scared. He threw the marula away. The elephant towering over Rurik began to eat the fruit that had fallen furthest from the tree. Now he looked content, but was always between Rurik and the fruit. Rurik was hungry and his fear diminished.

"And you couldn't eat those already on the ground. You had to half break the tree down to get at the fresh ones. What would you eat next year? In any case, it is your tree. You can do what you want, you glutton!" Rurik spoke accusingly.

Occasionally Emperor would fling a bad one away with his trunk. He ate only the best. There was a particularly tasty looking marula right in front of Emperor. He will definitely eat that one, Rurik thought. Emperor ate around the tasty looking fruit and almost passed over it. Maybe Rurik could get it later. Then slowly Emperor reached back with his trunk, picked it up and lifted it towards his mouth.

"You glutton. You'll have that one too," Rurik said disappointed.

Halfway up Emperor changed his mind and flung it away. It rolled and stopped right in front of Rurik, looking ripe and tasty.

"So you have decided, I can eat too. There are too many even for your big stomach. I don't know how you can eat so much. You have been stuffing yourself all day."

Rurik picked the fruit up and brought it to his mouth. It was rotten on the other side. He smiled at Emperor and they forgot the nonsense, too busy eating. They ate for most of the afternoon.

His hunger satisfied, Rurik rested against the tree. The marulas fermented in his stomach and the alcohol entered his bloodstream. Even Emperor had stopped eating, he looked very relaxed and swayed to and fro. The constant movement of the elephant's body was hypnotizing in its repetition and Rurik's eyes began to lose focus. His head was light and he was getting a headache. Slowly the body of the elephant faded as Rurik's vision blurred from the effects of the alcohol. Rurik wished he hadn't eaten so much fruit. He couldn't keep his eyes open and he slipped into a world of stupor. He fell asleep as darkness fell, and slept through the night but at dawn Rurik dreamed about Sandy and Kito.

They were playing on the rocks exposed by the low tide, while

Rurik sat in the shade enjoying the idyllic picture of mother and child. His heart was filled with happiness as he watched the two people he loved, healthy and happy. Kito was trying to trap a fish in the channel between the rocks and Sandy was goading him on. Full of life and still as beautiful as when they had first met, Sandy ran around chasing the fish in Kito's direction, while he screamed happily when the fish was within his reach. Rurik knew their chances of catching a fish were slim. They knew it too, but enjoyed playing in the late afternoon sun. That day they had had a picnic in the rocky bay and Rurik had enjoyed the red wine a little too much, so he had decided to sit in the shade and watch the magic scene. Waves were breaking far from the shore and white foam covered most of the bay. It was one of those perfect days when the weather, the relationships and the emotions were just right.

Rurik watched for a while, but couldn't resist the temptation to participate in the play. He was getting up to join in the activity, when the scream shattered his peace. He looked at Sandy, alarmed because it was her that had screamed and saw Kito running toward her.

"Don't come to me, don't come to me. Keep away," she screamed. The boy didn't listen. She stepped forward, screamed with pain and with great effort picked Kito up. Rurik ran to them. He couldn't understand the reason for Sandy's distress. The scene had been so idyllic. "What is wrong?" he shouted in panic, dread rising in his chest.

Sandy lifted her leg, stepped backwards and then turned to Rurik, clutching Kito firmly to her chest.

"I have stepped on a stone fish," she said, agony on her face.

Rurik saw the deadly creature lying at Sandy's feet, an evil rock with an upturned mouth, thirteen hollow spikes sticking from its back.

Sandy had stepped on it for a second time, on purpose, to protect their son, when Kito had run to her after she screamed. Rurik looked into the eyes he loved and saw terror and suffering.

He hugged his wife, knowing there was no hope. They were too far from any hospital. She was going to die. They were going to lose her. The thought devastated Rurik.

"No," he screamed and the scream changed his world.

10

<small>B</small>ewildered, heart pounding, blood rushing to his head, the scream echoing in his mind, Rurik stared at the Pel's fishing owl on the branch above. She screeched again. An unearthly sound that brought the fragmented pieces of three worlds together. The bay, amnesia and the present, kaleidoscoped into one unhappy world. Kito! Where is he? Is he alive? Rurik's heart cried.

He had been absent for days. No doubt there had been a renewed attack of malaria and there was no one to nurse his boy. Kito could be dead. If his son was dead Rurik had to know, he had to bury him, so the wild animals would not scatter his bones across the swamp. No, he had to think positive.

How would he find his way back to Kito? A movement in the bush distracted Rurik's thoughts and he saw a squirrel next to the elephant's ear. She appeared to be in animated discussion, while the elephant seemed grumpy and annoyed. He probably felt like Rurik: heavy and sluggish with a confused mind.

Rurik recalled his following the elephant and realized that his childish naivety and desperate need for friendship had outweighed his fear of the animal. Nevertheless, he felt friendship toward the giant. The elephant had brought Rurik here to the place where he had regained his memory. Perhaps, by some divine providence, he would take him back to his son.

He couldn't be too far from Kito, Rurik thought. He had been wandering in the bush for three days, but had not walked in a straight line. It was possible that Kito could be an hour away, but probably no more than a day.

The flight of a bird captured Rurik's attention. A Pels fishing owl was a rare bird. Perhaps the tree by their camp was its home. Maybe it was flying home. It was the only probability Rurik had.

He turned to follow the owl and cast a last glance at the elephant who slowly raised his head and hooked a branch with his curved tusk. The gash in the shape of a bow was clearly visible and Rurik wondered how he had earned it.

The elephant's eyes looked sad as Rurik waved goodbye. Even the squirrel stopped chattering. With a sense of loss, he followed the owl. After a while he spotted her again. It seemed that if he walked in the general direction of the owl's flight he would always find her again. He followed the bird for hours and then she disappeared. Rurik wondered if he should have stayed with the elephant. The elephant always eventually came to the water and Kito was by the water.

Rurik walked on, using the sun as a guide. His thirst reminded him that he had to find water. Was Kito alive? Where was he? It seemed unlikely now that Rurik would find him. Why had he come to the swamp? He had been foolish to think that they could forget Sandy's death. The dream had been a vivid reminder of the tragedy. He would never forget her agony and pain, nor could he forget the magic moments they had shared. The other picture which would forever remain etched in his memory was the catamaran in flames, sailing over the breakers, Sandy's body lying on the pyre they had built from driftwood, and her ashes being scattered above the reef, as the catamaran sank.

Rurik walked on, hoping to spot the owl, his desperation growing with each passing hour. He was hopelessly lost. He would never see his son again. Despondent, he stumbled on. Then he saw the clearing. He ran toward the majestic tree guarding the entrance to their camp, his heart beating furiously as doubt and terrible anxiety squeezed his chest. He felt both hope and dread.

Rurik ran past the giant and along the animal path. He saw the thorn wall and a wisp of smoke at the same time and his heart jumped with joy. Kito must be well. As he ran past the last bushes, Rurik saw Kito lying motionless on the bed of grass, sweat on his forehead. The attack had come again.

The door of the enclosure was open and some brownish concoction was brewing in the pot. Rurik ran to Kito, kneeled and gently touched his son as if to make sure he was real. He hugged the boy, tears welling up in his eyes. He thanked God for bringing him back to his son, and guiding another person to help Kito in his absence. Who was it that was making the brew?

Instinctively, Rurik turned around and through his tears saw an old man. He stood like an apparition at the entrance of the enclosure, a fish in one hand and a small spear in the other. A bow and quiver were on his back and a knife on his hip. He looked frail but his eyes shone with great inner strength.

Rurik walked to the old man, his hand outstretched. "You have saved my son. Thank you. If I can do anything for you I will gladly do it. Whatever it is. I am in eternal debt to you. Everything I have is yours."

"I am glad I could help your son. You don't owe me anything. I have what I need." He replied in accented, but perfect English.

"Take my knife." Rurik unbuckled his belt to take the sheath off.

"You need a knife and I have a knife. What would I do with two knives? At my age any additional weight would only be a burden. I have already been rewarded by finding you and the boy." The old man's eyes examined Rurik's as if searching for something.

"His name is Kito, and I am Rurik," Rurik said wondering what reward the old man was talking about.

"He told me his name. You named the boy appropriately. He is a jewel. Precious," the old man said. Kito groaned and Rurik swung around but the boy was still motionless as he was a moment ago.

"Will he be all right?" Rurik asked.

"Kito is strong, but the fever is also strong. This potion contains the bark of the Quinine tree; it is good medicine and will help the boy fight. He stands a good chance," the old man said. He poured some of the brew into a bark container and blew, cooling it, then carefully he poured it into Kito's mouth.

"Thank you again. I am deeply indebted to you. I wish I could do something to repay my debt, although I know I could never repay it in full. Kito is all I have and without him my life would be meaningless," Rurik said, his voice filled with emotion as he looked intently at the old man.

"The depth of your love for your son is payment enough, but there is something I will ask of you."

"Whatever it is I'll gladly do it," Rurik said eagerly.

"It will occupy your whole life and your son's life. It is a task that requires sacrifice and a continuous battle." The old man watched Rurik earnestly.

"I owe you a great debt, so I will commit myself, but I cannot commit my son. He has to be free to make his own choices." Rurik spoke with conviction, but there was also caution in his voice.

"Even if you wanted, you couldn't commit your son. Embarking on the road I am proposing has to come from inner conviction and not from coercion. But it is a noble task, a task which would bring great rewards to you, your son and mankind if you succeed." The old man's voice, calm and even, matched the serenity of his face.

"What is it you are asking?" Rurik asked.

"You have to save the wilderness of the world," the old man said, without a change of expression or tone of voice.

In astonishment Rurik looked at the old man. He couldn't believe it. He searched the old man's face to see whether or not he was teasing but saw only a serious and composed expression.

"How can I save the wilderness? Many people have tried but destruction is still happening at an incredible rate. Soon there will be no wilderness."

Rurik lifted his hands in a gesture of helplessness, hoping he looked convincing enough to convey that he was taking the proposal seriously. It seemed as though he had succeeded because the old man continued in the same tone of voice.

"The fate of humankind is tied to the fate of the wilderness. First you must understand how critically important for your and your son's future it is to change the collective mind of mankind in a direction that would benefit the preservation and restitution of the wilderness and wild life."

The old man spoke solemnly and forcefully. He did make sense in his analysis of the consequences of the present trend, but he definitely didn't make sense when he asked Rurik to change it.

"I know how important it is to preserve our natural heritage, but what can I do? I am one man. I am prepared to commit my life to a viable idea and am very happy to listen, but I seriously doubt one is able to change the direction in which the world is going."

Expectantly Rurik looked at the old wise eyes. He saw hesitation and then determination. They seemed to see Rurik's innermost thoughts and Rurik worried that the old man would see what he was thinking. Eyes still focussed on Rurik, the old man continued, "This world was created on the basis of the interdependence of all life upon it. An antelope eats grass and in turn it fertilizes the grass. Man eats the antelope so he is dependent on the antelope and the grass. In the ocean, fish eat the plankton and man eats the fish. Every day there are more men, less fish and less antelope. Every day deserts become bigger and forests smaller. Soon there will be too many men, too little grass, and too few animals and fish. The trees create oxygen, and if the number of trees and men are disproportional, we will use more oxygen than the trees produce and the weak will die. Nature keeps things in balance so men will die until the numbers become proportional again. The balance will be re-established but at great cost and great suffering. The fittest will survive but will become savages; the strong will kill the weak in order to preserve for themselves the little that is left. The world will be hell."

Fascinated by the simplicity of the old man's logic Rurik looked at his sober face and clearly saw the frightening future. He knew the world was going in the wrong direction but never before had he been able to see the consequences so starkly. He looked at Kito's sweaty face and realized that Kito or Kito's children might face the kind of future the old man was talking about. Perhaps he knew the way, however incredible his proposal sounded.

Rurik looked at the old man again and with trepidation in his voice he said, "I am only one man. The task is enormous and seems impossible."

"Rurik, do you know that all the islands in the Okavango are made by termites?"

"Yes, I do, but it took thousands of years." Rurik almost shouted, exasperated.

"Each one of them was started with one wet particle moved in the darkness by two lonely termites. Then another grain followed and soon passageways and galleries were made. Two ordinary termites became king and queen and they bred. Then the seeds took in the rich soil and the first young tree sprang from the mound. Even if the queen dies it is replaced by another queen and the colony lives on. If the queen doesn't lay eggs she is eaten by the other termites and is replaced by another queen. You too, could start an island, an island of sanity. If your base is sound, more people who care will leave the sea of insanity and join in your effort. Your island will grow."

Rurik was astounded by the task the old man was asking him to undertake. He had only ever fought for his own immediate concerns and never for wider issues. This he had always left to somebody else, despite his awareness that some people got involved in conservation and other activities for personal gain and popularity and not out of conviction. He condemned their morality, but had never become involved in trying to influence a change in society. He had opted out, and the old man's words made it clear to him how selfish and short-sighted his life had been.

"Where should I start?" he asked. "Not that I think I can succeed."

The old man's face crinkled in a smile, his eyes were warm and accepting.

"You start by understanding your objective. Your objective is to change man. He was given a free mind and is capable of rapid change. Man was also given intellect to create tools. He has used his intellect to create engines and make his life easier, but has not used them responsibly. He has over-rated his own importance and under-rated the importance of other species. He has replaced spirituality with materialism and from a natural world he has created an unnatural environment. Your task is to reverse the trend. Spirituality must grow in importance and materialism lessen."

The fervor of his speech had visibly drained the old man's energy, the vein on his temple was more prominent and his face seemed older.

"That is impossible. Nobody is going to listen. Materialism has been growing over centuries and it's at its height." Rurik was beginning to sympathize with the old man's frustration, but still, he didn't see a viable solution to the problem.

"It is good that materialism is at its height. Everything declines from its height, so will materialism. It has caused suffering, uncertainty and unhappiness which is widespread between the rich and the poor. If man doesn't shoulder the responsibility he has been given, the suffering, uncertainty and unhappiness will grow and there will be no peace. You begin by telling this to the world." The last words the old man spoke aggressively.

"How do I make people listen to me? I am nobody and have no audience. I have isolated myself from society for years. I have no platform from which to speak." Frustration was evident in Rurik's voice.

"When we are born we are helpless but as we grow we learn something new everyday. I am an old man but I am still learning. You are young and your son is even younger. Between you, you have much time to learn and do. Your audience need not be numerous. Seek wise men and they will help you make your audience bigger. Every great journey begins with a decision."

Rurik knew this. He had expressed the same sentiment to Kito, except he had spoken of one man and the old man was speaking about mankind. Did it make a difference? Didn't everything work on the same principle? Miyamoto Musashi the greatest sword fighter of his time in "The Book of Five Rings", wrote in the early sixteen hundreds that if one is able to fight one man, one is able to fight ten men. Rurik didn't really understand this, but as he gazed at the still waters of the lagoon he felt that here in this wilderness, where he had learned so much, he was about to learn much, much more.

If everything worked on the same principle, one man or the whole of mankind, it wouldn't make any difference. Rurik found it difficult to control his own actions, so how then does one man influence mankind? How does one reconcile the contrasting values of humanity with its diverse cultures and conflicting needs?

Rurik was astounded, the old man's vision struck a chord and coincided with his own yearnings. From a dreamer he was being asked to become a doer. But how could he undertake a task beyond his ability? Bewildered by his conflicting sentiments, Rurik tried to compose his thoughts, and finally he spoke.

"How can I undertake a task I cannot be sure I can execute? I am a good advertising man, but nothing out of the ordinary. I would have to fight the entrenched forces of greed, ego and poverty, with enormous influence and control over society. An industrialist destroys forests for profit, so he can buy rhino's horn or elephant's tusk - symbols of power and wealth. A person who kills a rhino or chops down a tree is enticed to do so by money and poverty, while governments pass or maintain laws that allow the industrialist to destroy the forests because the government gets a share of profits through taxes. These are forces against which I have no chance. Others have tried."

"Did these others have any success?" asked the old man.

"Some of them achieved limited success, but nobody can stop this destruction driven by values entrenched in the fibres of society." Rurik's voice was frustrated and helpless.

The old man stood up, took the bark container, poured some brew into it and held it in both hands while he squatted looking at the fire. Rurik wiped Kito's face. Kito was sweating less and his face had regained some of its natural color. Rurik wished his son would regain consciousness.

"It is essential to change the values, and then everything would change," Rurik heard the old man say and turned to look at him as he continued.

"If you can show people that a change of values would benefit them, they would embrace those values and you would achieve success." The old man spoke with conviction.

"But materialism is the only value that is worshipped," Rurik said. He stopped for a moment and then continued bitterly, "Materialism is what has brought the world to the state in which it is today. The manufacturers continuously glorify virtues of material wealth through the media and people are being convinced that only by obtaining material possessions, can they enter the upper echelons of society and be respected. It is natural for man to crave respect and the easy life. To convince him to change is nearly impossible. You have to offer something more," Rurik was sweating now.

The old man looked at the frustrated Rurik. In an even voice he said, "It is *nearly* impossible, but not impossible. Every man that has fought for conservation has achieved some success, however small. All successes add up, they have not reversed the trend, but they have slowed down the rate of destruction and have gained time by delaying extinction. I was once associated with a man who did a great job in the conservation of the Okavango and Africa. His name was Dr. Adams."

"Yes, I have heard of Dr. Adams. He fought successfully to ban the trade in ivory and rhino horn. His death shocked and enraged the world. The details of his work and achievements were widely covered by the media world-wide."

"Dr.Adams is dead?" The old man's eyes clouded and his face showed pain.

"Yes, he was killed by poachers. How were you associated with him?"

The old man looked at the brew in his hands which shook almost imperceptibly. Rurik saw the sorrow on his face and felt deep sympathy for this man who had saved his son.

"I worked with him," the old man said in a subdued voice. "He was a great man. In the twenty seven years of our association he opened my eyes to a wider picture of the world. Maybe if I had stayed he would not now be dead. Many times I guided him away from the dangers of the bush. When was he killed?"

"About six months ago. They found his body riddled by bullets, next to the carcasses of six elephants. Their tusks were hacked off. You must then be the one they called Madala—The Old Man!" Rurik almost shouted the last sentence.

"Yes, I am Madala."

"This is unbelievable! I have read so much about you and your disappearance. When nobody saw you for so many years everybody thought you were dead. Dr.Adams always spoke about you being his teacher, the one who taught him about animal behavior and their needs. Your disappearance became a tragic example of the disillusionment and annihilation of a breed of people who had understood Africa, and had preserved it by living in harmony with other species for thousands of years. Dr.Adams portrayed you as the embodiment of a beautiful Africa which changed to a place of suffering and desperation. I am so honored I have met you."

Madala stood up slowly, sadness apparent in the way he held his body, grief reflected in his solemn face. He walked over to Kito and carefully poured the potion into his mouth. When Kito had drunk all of the medicine, Madala put his hand on Kito's forehead and held it there, as if his hand was receiving and interpreting life forces. He said to Rurik, "I think, soon, the boy is going to wake up."

Rurik's heart leaped with excitement and his body felt light with happiness. He longed to see his son healthy, and see the clear eyes of his boy full of life again.

Rurik watched Madala walk slowly to the water where he stood looking into the distance. Madala stood at the water edge mourning the death of his friend and, Rurik assumed, the death of the conviction which gave an animal a chance. Rurik still found it difficult to believe that this man was the mystical Madala. He was famous throughout the world, without even knowing it. This old, frail and simple man, with almost no possessions, had achieved unparalleled success by understanding the world in which he lived and by passing his knowledge on to others. He and Dr.Adams had reversed the depletion of elephants in Botswana. They had changed the course of extinction to such an extent that the elephant population had so increased in numbers that, due to the inability to migrate, they faced death from starvation. Man had erected barriers along the elephant's migratory routes, denying to him what every man held as his God given right, *freedom and prosperity*. The elephant was jailed in the land which belonged to him, his life being his only crime.

Rurik wiped the beads of sweat from Kito's forehead, stood up and resolutely walked to Madala. The old man turned at the sound of Rurik's footsteps, sadness etched in every wrinkle of his face. His grief touched Rurik's heart and his resolve strengthened. He stood in front of the old man, towering above the frail figure. He looked directly into Madala's eyes and said, "Madala, teach me and I will dedicate my life to fighting for justice in this world. Dr.Adams achieved so much through your teaching, perhaps I can do it too. I am willing to try."

A spark of anticipation broke through the resignation in Madala's eyes and he straightened his wiry body. In a determined voice he said, "If you are willing to learn, then I am willing to teach you everything I know. I will die in peace if I pass my experiences onto you, for then I have fulfilled my mission." Madala's voice was filled with emotion.

"Now let's go and prepare the fish. Kito will need to eat when he wakes up and so do we. We'll need to get some fruit and honey to help him regain the energy he has lost." The old face wrinkled into a smile and Madala's eyes radiated love as he mentioned Kito.

As he walked with Madala, Rurik's excitement grew at the prospect of being guided by this great man. His belief in victory over forces of destruction leaped. This man and Dr. Adams had initiated the move to conserve the elephant and succeeded in bringing about the first major reversal in the pattern of destruction of wildlife. Rurik thought it significant that two men, one white and one black, united by a common goal had achieved such success and realized how daunting the task must have seemed at its inception. Their achievement inspired Rurik, giving him new perspective. He was suddenly aware of what men of this caliber could accomplish. He *had* to become one of these men. From the entrance of the enclosure he looked at his son who had almost no sweat on his face now. Rurik smiled, convinced that he could face the challenge.

Madala cleaned the fish while Rurik rekindled the fire and made a small spit. When Madala was finished he gave the fish to Rurik and poured some more potion into Kito's mouth, again feeling the boy's forehead.

"Kito will be with us soon," he said as he sat down across the fire from Rurik. "He is fighting exceptionally well, you must have invested much time and thought in his upbringing for him to be so strong."

Rurik smiled, and proudly looking at his son he spoke.

"His mother and I raised him in a bay just south of the Mozambican border. We taught him to live according to natural principles, and not to adopt artificial values prevalent in the modern world. We emphasized the importance of true self assessment hoping to eliminate the danger that an unrealistic self-assessment brings. We tried to balance his need for mental and physical development. We took him to see man's great achievements. We travelled to see St Peter's Basilica, the pyramids and the Louvre and showed him the natural wonders of the world. We read to him from the great books and told him about God. He was allowed freedom in accordance with his ability to understand the responsibility which comes with it. Our perceptions often clashed on this subject, but our love frequently facilitated compromise. A smack on the backside was used in facilitating an argument when love failed." A quick smile crossed Rurik's face before he continued.

"In teaching the boy we learned ourselves. We tried to live in accordance with our teaching. We didn't always succeed. In spite of the fact that we studied philosophy and followed the changes of thinking over millennia it was not easy to live an exemplary life. We also studied marine life and astronomy and the boy was always present. We taught him that freedom has its responsibilities, that man loses his freedom if he enslaves another and that freedom is a state of mind, as is slavery. We looked for his natural inclinations and encouraged their development, told him that failure and success are relative to the individual's perception, and avoided the tendency to direct the boy to pursue our aims instead of his. We believed that he should be what his natural inclinations led him to be." Rurik looked at Madala who sat listening attentively, and encouraged, Rurik continued.

"We enrolled him in a correspondence school so options would be open if he decided to return to the industrial society. We taught him to speak the truth so his mind wouldn't be saturated with devising infertile schemes to justify his lies. He responded eagerly and developed into a strong and natural boy. He contributed to the household by catching crabs from which we made soup, or by collecting driftwood for the fire. He speared his first fish when he was eight and we made supper a celebration. Yes, we brought him up as best we could and were very proud of him."

While Rurik talked, the spark in Madala's eyes grew in intensity. "You have done a good job and you *should* be proud," he said.

"Your most important mission is to care for, and teach your child.

Together you two can face any task you choose and bring it to a successful conclusion. I can see that you have been bewildered by recent events in your life: your wife's death and your son's illness. You temporarily lost your belief in the future, but it is good to go through trials. Trials make you re-examine your direction and re-adjust your vision. The more you think, the clearer your goals become. Clarity always comes after confusion and gives you renewed energy to pursue your vision. Your belief in the vision of an ideal world will enable you to bring it about, in spite of the formidable obstacles you will undoubtedly encounter."

"Dad," a weak voice came from behind Rurik. He jumped to his feet and spun around.

"My boy! You are awake." His voice trembled with excitement.

Rurik embraced and kissed his son and looked at his green eyes, wanting to imprint them forever into his soul.

"I am so happy to see you again. I was worried about you," Kito said weakly. "I love you, Dad. I thought I would never see you again."

"I love you too my son, more than ever. I am sorry I made you worry, but everything is all right now."

Kito's weak smile spread happiness over his face and lightened his eyes.

"You have been gone long," he said.

"I fell and knocked my head and when I regained consciousness I did not know who I was, or where I was. Then I regained my memory and found my way back. What happened to you after I left?"

"I was fine in the morning, but in the afternoon I became worried that something had happened to you. I felt cold and I knew the fever was coming again so I took two anti-malaria tablets and put wood on the fire. It didn't help and I became delirious. Once I felt somebody pouring some bitter tasting liquid down my throat and I thought you were back, but when I opened my eyes I saw an old man standing above me. The liquid tasted terrible but made me feel better. I asked him about you and he told me that you would come back. Where is Madala now?"

"I am here Kito. You fought well. You are a strong boy and now I have some good fish for you to make you even stronger," said Madala and showed Kito the almost ready fish on the spit.

"Madala, I am not hungry. How did you know my Dad was going to come back?"

"I'll tell you some other time, but you'll have to eat. You need to eat in order to recover fast. If you are weak, I won't be able to teach you to pole the mokoro and hunt as I promised."

Kito ate a little and soon he fell asleep again.

Madala wouldn't allow Kito to be awakened for medicine. "He must sleep. That is the best medicine," he said with finality. Rurik could see in Madala's eyes that he liked Kito and was drawn to him.

During the days that followed, Rurik told Kito and Madala about his adventures with the elephant. Kito was amazed by Rurik's experience and couldn't stop asking questions. Madala however, thought it was nothing extraordinary. He was convinced that the Spirit of the swamp had guided Rurik, the elephant and the owl, as he guides every other living thing.

A week later, when Kito was able to stand, all three of them walked to the clearing together. In the days that followed Madala told them about the swamp. He taught them how to catch lizards, gather ants, which water lilies made a good stew and how to prepare all of them. They learned eagerly. Rurik had many discussions with Madala about his mission but Madala paid special attention to Kito. Rurik was almost jealous of the affection Kito received, even though he was very proud that his son attracted so much attention from a man such as Madala.

One day Madala was particularly pleased with Kito's progress in tracking. That evening Kito asked Rurik to tell him about Emperor when Madala interrupted.

"Kito, I have seen this elephant not far from here, just before I saw the smoke of your fire. Maybe the elephant is still in the area, although the bulls do wander over long distances. Elephants love marulas so he might have stayed. Maybe we could try to track him down."

"Please Madala, take us there. I would love to see Emperor," said Kito excitedly. Madala agreed.

Dawn was just breaking when they pushed the mokoro into the water and two hours later they moored at the place where Madala had seen the elephant. He searched for tracks alongside the water but had no success. Kito was disappointed and urged Madala to look some more. They crossed the plain and as they came close to the forest Rurik spotted the baobab tree, which he had mistaken for the tree by their camp. From there he knew the general direction in which he and the elephant had moved and guided them to the place where they had drunk water after eating the marulas. Madala found tracks of the elephant here and followed them to the marula tree where they ate a couple of fruits which they found among the broken branches. Madala walked in ever increasing circles, until he found tracks about three days old going south, which they followed. Kito screeched with excitement and Rurik felt ebullient with expectation.

Kito asked Madala how he knew that the tracks were three days old. Madala explained that the sharpness of the spoor edges, the freshness of the small mounds of soil which insects had dug in the imprints and the state of the huge piles of dung they encountered alongside the spoor were all indicators. The track led them out of the forest and onto the plain and after a while Madala stopped.

"The elephant is gone," he said. "He will walk for days now before he settles in an area again."

"How do you know he will walk for days?" Kito asked, disappointed that his expectations of meeting the elephant, which in his mind was the epitome of greatness, were dashed.

"He walked without stopping or hesitating, you can see the indentations are evenly spaced. He passed by the tree whose leaves he loves to eat, and didn't even stop to drink water. He has definitely decided to go. We have no chance of catching up to him. We would have to walk for days, maybe weeks, to find him."

They were all disappointed, but Kito looked devastated and Madala tried to console him.

"Kito, the elephant is heading south. There is a chance that you might meet him on your way, but if you don't, do something for him and his kind, to repay your debt." Madala said compassionately.

"What can I do for an elephant?"

"You can ensure that he has the space he needs to wander," interjected Rurik.

"How?"

"You have to fight for it," Rurik said resolutely.

"Dad if you show me how, I will fight for your elephant."

Rurik put his arm around Kito's shoulder and both of them looked down the endless plain, determination on their faces.

"I will show you my son," Rurik tightened his grip.

"We have to go back if we are to get to the camp before dark," Madala's voice brought them out of the momentary entrancement and they followed the old man in silence.

They reached camp as the last light was fading and Madala made the fire. Everybody was disappointed at not finding the elephant. The silent faces stared at the flames until Kito pushed a half burned piece of wood into the fire and looked at his father. "How do we fight for the elephant's space?" he asked.

Rurik tried to compose his thoughts. He looked at Kito and turned to Madala, seeking help. The old man sensed Rurik's confusion and readily answered.

"You have to fight the arrogance of man."

"How do you fight arrogance?"

"Arrogance is the belief that man is self-dependant and all-deserving while all other species are at his disposal. Arrogance is not understanding that man is dependant on other life as much as that life is dependant on man. You must tell this to other men and plead with them to give the elephant the space which he needs to survive."

"But would people listen to me? Why don't the three of us do it together?" Kito asked. "You are coming with us, aren't you?"

"No, I cannot go with you. I am an old man and I would like to die here where I was born. This is my world. I'll take you out of the swamp and go back to my people. You don't need me. You have a commitment and over the last few weeks I have told you everything I think is important. You can succeed. I would just be a burden. Tomorrow we'll practice mokoro poling. You still push the pole too deep."

The old man stood up slowly, supporting himself on his spear. "Good night" he said and walked into the grass hut.

"Dad, we must not leave Madala alone. We must persuade him to come with us," Kito whispered to Rurik.

"Kito we'll stay for a few more days and try to convince Madala to come with us and maybe he will change his mind." Rurik whispered.

"I can't wait till tomorrow to pole the mokoro. It is such fun." Kito said.

The following day they poled south. Rurik and Kito alternated at the pole and Madala explained to them the route they would have to take to get back to civilization. In the evening he spoke about the Okavango and his life.

Mostly he spoke about the places he had seen and interesting things he had learned about animals. He had learned from the leopard and vulture, from the snake and eagle. In a trembling voice he recounted the thirteen months over which twenty three earthquakes had shaken the Okavango, causing the Boro river, dry for thirty years, to flow again. He told them about old rivers that died and new streams being born, about his youth and how women extracted perfume from dried grass stems and how, side by side, they scooped fish with woven baskets.

He reminisced about underwater gardens, consisting of plants with many colored stems, red and gold and pale green and waiting for the floods which each year changed direction and left last years inlets dry. His voice rose, revering termites which built structures up to eight meters high and cultivated tiny mushrooms on their excretions. He told them how they were genetically prevented from breeding, until flying had occurred. That forced the termites to build new nests away from the old ones and avoid overcrowding, he explained.

He told them that giraffes had a special valve in their necks so that blood does not rush to the brain when they bend down to drink.

With his words he weaved a picture of himself making fishing nets from fibres of the wild plants and poisoning the fish in shallow pools by throwing in dried ground bark of the Matsebe tree, and about the prayer he said every time he killed an animal, asking for forgiveness.

"This was the world," Madala said, "in which there were no conservation laws, where everybody hunted freely and in which there were always plenty of animals, because there was one law everyone obeyed: *No man will take more than he needs. To take more is a sin.*" Kito and Rurik were fascinated and learned how this kind of restraint could assure the future of the world.

On the third day when they went into the swamp again, Rurik asked Madala to go with them and tell people his fascinating story about the incredible world into which he had been born. Madala replied that Rurik and Kito knew the story and now they must speak. He didn't have time, for the Spirit of the swamp was calling him. Kito, almost an expert now, poled on the way back, his body swaying with superb co-ordination as he pushed the pole into the water.

The old man looked very tired and frail that evening and both Rurik and Kito were subdued as they sat around the fire.

"Please Madala, come with us," Kito pleaded.

For a long time Madala looked at the fire, his features calm, his wise eyes beaming peace and then as if he had made a decision he started talking.

"For seven years I have wandered through the swamp looking for peace and atonement for my sins. I kept away from any humans and searched for the Spirit to confess my sins and ask for forgiveness. One day I felt my time had come but I was not afraid of death. I had to find the Great Spirit of the swamp so my spirit could find a home. I knew this would be my last search. If I didn't find peace my spirit would wander. I saw a Sitatunga being killed by a crocodile and that incident made me realize that I had neglected my duty to help prevent the destruction of my world. I decided to go back and in the little time I had left do what I had neglected doing for seven years. When I saw the smoke of your fire I had a strange feeling of accomplishment and wondered why. I found Kito and I saw that he was near death. I asked the spirit of the tree to help the boy and gave him the potion. The spirit obliged and for the first time in seven years, or maybe even thirty seven, through Kito, I felt I had communicated with the Spirit again and I felt peace for the first time. I sensed that the boy was one of nature's children and that he could restore the balance again, if I planted a seed in him. I knew then that there was an eternity of time for the idea to grow and my vision to be realized. For the first time in over thirty years I experienced true happiness."

When Madala stopped, the crackling of the fire was the only sound in the enclosure for a long time. Kito finally broke the silence.

"How are you going to find the spirit you have been looking for?" he asked.

Madala looked at Kito and smiled. "I have found the place and I have found peace," he said.

In the morning Madala was dead. They buried him at the foot of the baobab tree, knowing that his spirit would become one with the spirit of the tree. The two ancient spirits would combine to reach the Great Spirit of the swamp.

Solemnly they stood by the grave. Kito had fashioned a cross from carefully chosen branches of a young tree and positioned it at the head of the grave. Rurik wondered what Kito was thinking as he stood next to the grave with his head bowed, occasionally wiping his eyes with the back of his hand. Rurik saw tears in his eyes and tried to comfort him, but Kito's grief was deep and Rurik had no success.

Rurik asked God to forgive Madala's sins and not to burden his spirit with the wrongs he had committed in ignorance. As he closed his eyes in prayer, a picture of steely blue eyes emerged from the depths of his mind. He looked at the mound again, astounded by the thought that Madala might be the spirit of his father. The vision of steely eyes was in his mind throughout the day and that night he dreamed about the unspoiled hills of his youth.

11

The following days on the water, Kito and his father spoke little, still influenced by Madala's death. His father was quiet and thoughtful and it made Kito worry. He was also preoccupied by the problem of getting out of the swamp. In the month they spent with Madala, Kito had forgotten that they were in an unknown environment.

When his father was not poling, he sat in the front of the mokoro and stared into the distance. When he spoke to Kito, he spoke in a listless voice and his eyes had an unsettled look. Kito wouldn't be worried about getting out of the swamp if his father didn't look so thoughtful and worried. Madala had taught them how to live off the swamp and they also had his weapons and net. They had some honey and dried snake meat. Madala had told them that it would take about a week to get to an inhabited area, but that they might meet people before; tourists and hunters frequented the southern part of the swamp. Twice already they had taken channels which led them to a dead end. Kito hoped that today they wouldn't repeat the mistakes of the previous two days.

He had only seen his father like this after his mom had died. That was the only time his father had been withdrawn and didn't talk to him the way he usually did. Kito remembered how uncertain his father had been about what to do and how very insecure Kito had felt.

Kito didn't like Johannesburg. He had missed the bay and all the space and freedom. There were too many people and the air was foul from exhaust fumes. The air bothered Kito and made him sluggish and lethargic.

Those three months were the unhappiest days of his life. Often he had asked if they shouldn't go back to the bay, but his father wouldn't talk about it.

Now, his father again looked as miserable as he had been before they decided to undertake this trip and Kito knew he was trying to make a difficult decision. His eyes were dull and his movements slow. Kito felt uneasy and uncertain.

That evening, after they had eaten and were sitting around the fire his father suddenly changed. He looked at Kito and smiled, his eyes clear and his shoulders straight. Kito knew he had made a decision about whatever was worrying him.

"Kito, I want to talk to you about something really important, so you must listen carefully. It is my responsibility to guide you in the direction which will achieve three objectives. The first is that you live a happy life. The other two are prerequisites for the first. The second is that you have a skill which will make you self-sufficient, so you can earn your living, and the third is to have an objective which will give your life meaning and be beneficial to your children. You must understand that we are not here just to exist, but that there has to be a mission for us as individuals, and for us as mankind.

"I cannot make the choice of what direction your life should take, although I can influence your thinking."

Startled by the abrupt change in sentiment and apparent urgency with which his dad was talking, Kito just stared as his dad continued.

"This is what has been going through my mind for the last three days. We'll soon be back in the "real" world and we both have to decide on the objective which will direct our future. After careful consideration of all factors I have decided to ask you something. I don't know if I have the right to ask, but if you decide against my proposal I will not try to change your mind. I must warn you, the road I am going to propose isn't an easy one, but then there are no easy roads in life."

"I knew you were thinking about something important but I was a little bit worried because Madala isn't with us anymore. I was not sure we would find a way out of the swamp," Kito said with relief, seeing that his father was back to normal.

"Don't worry Kito. All we have to do is go south and we will come to places that tourists frequent. Madala explained to me where we were and even if it takes us longer than a week to get there we are able to feed ourselves. Don't worry. We were in a much worse position before and we managed then. We still have to be careful about the dangers of the swamp, but even for those we are better prepared now after learning from Madala. We are both strong and we will survive and find our way."

Kito felt good, because his father was so definite in his statements. When he was like that Kito never worried.

"Dad I am not worried anymore," he said. "What were you going to ask me?"

"Kito, you have heard Madala talking about the wild and how important wildlife is for man's existence. Madala made me understand how critically important conservation is and the consequences of mankind continuing on its present course. It is vital that we actively contribute to the effort of conservation. I am asking you to make it your third objective. I will."

"Do you know what we have to do?" Kito asked.

"We have to make a plan of action for our lifetime and a plan for beyond.

"How can we make a plan for after our lifetime?" Kito knew his father would have an answer.

"It is simple," he said. "A child is the key. You are almost thirty years younger than I am. If everything works as it naturally should, then you will live more than thirty years longer than I. If I have an aim and we work toward it together, you would continue after my death, my ideas would be taken into the future and would live beyond my physical life. You would, of course, develop your own aims which would reach further than mine and your children would take them beyond your death. This could continue for generations if our ideas are based on right principles and are regularly adapted to suit changing times. Each new generation would do a better job."

"Why?"

"We are all a product of the society in which we live and our philosophy of life is shaped by current values. If I succeeded in influencing you to adopt better values you would be further ahead in your thinking than I was at your age. You would have learned from my experience and you would not make the mistakes I have made."

"What mistakes have you made?"

"The biggest mistake I have made was leaving society. When I became aware that social values were not beneficial to human happiness, I should have tried to influence change. Not run away. I now realize that we are part of a closed physical and emotional system. No one can escape earth and the consequences of our combined actions."

"I don't agree with you. When we lived in the bay we were happy and went into society when we wanted. How could what is happening in the world affect us?" Kito said convinced that his dad was wrong.

"Maybe it wouldn't have affected me so much, because the country was wild and the roads were dirt tracks. There was enough fish in the sea for us to feed ourselves. But society builds roads and pollutes the oceans and with time our bay would have become easily accessible, then polluted, then the fish would be gone. You would definitely have faced this situation by the time you were my age and your child would have had no choice but to adjust to the inflow of masses, or move away to look for another isolated spot.

Even if your child did find another spot it wouldn't remain isolated for longer than a generation. We cannot escape being a part of society. Look at the disappearing Aral sea in Asia, which is about as big as Ireland. Activities thousands of kilometers away are making it shrink. Soon it will be gone if something isn't done urgently."

Kito's perception of the world gained a new dimension and again he thought about the three months he had lived in Johannesburg. From his new perspective the world didn't look like the endless space he had imagined before, but a small globe overcrowded with people. He had thought that the bay would never change. But when he imagined it being like Cape Town beach, he became sad.

"What can we do so this does not happen?" he asked with urgency.

"We have to restrict population growth."

"How do we do that?"

"By education. Kito, on this we have to take a long term view, so we start with the child. If a child is taught properly, the child will accept the principles of balance without difficulty and grow in harmony with nature. If we concentrated our efforts into education we would resolve the problem."

"All children go to school and get education. Why didn't this happen before?"

Rurik looked at Kito as if he was surprised by his statement and then to correct the misconception he said. "You are wrong. There are millions of children who don't go to school. Those that do are influenced by the prevailing values which are wrong. Also these children spend most of their time separated from their working parents, which for the child is unnatural. For a child to develop naturally it needs a proper environment."

"What is a proper environment?"

"The most important environment for a child is the family environment. Over the last fifty years the family has been destroyed at the same rate as the environment. You see the connection? A degenerating family produces children living by wrong values and society and nature deteriorates. In increasing numbers, adults are arising from broken families and are in many cases destructive.

"The family is the basic unit of society. If the family is sound, society will be sound. In a sound society a child will grow with sound principles and create a progressively better society."

This was upsetting Kito. He was frightened by the prospect of a world which was becoming progressively worse.

"How do you make a good family?" he asked.

"You make a good family by love. When you love your child you do what is best for the child's future and that is to live in a better world. In order to create a better world a parent would sacrifice some luxuries and conserve the natural resources for his child. Foregoing these luxuries would give parents more time to spend teaching their child."

"If I had a family and did what you say, but others continued doing whatever they were doing now, it wouldn't make any difference. There are millions of families in the world. How do you change all of them? It is impossible."

Kito was frustrated by failing to perceive a clear line of action and frightened by the feeling that change was not possible. He hoped his father had an answer, but he doubted it, because the whole thing sounded so complicated.

"Nothing is impossible. That is the first thing you have to believe. Secondly, anything you want to do has to start somewhere. In this case you have to start by changing your own values. Don't look at other people's faults. Look at your own faults and the values by which you live. Once you have changed, you will be able to change those around you. The more recognition you gain for your achievements, the more people will follow your philosophy."

"Which are the values you are talking about?"

"First of all you must be humble. You saw Madala, he was a great man, but always humble. You must teach your children to be humble too."

Something was wrong here, Kito thought, while he looked at

the fire. His Dad had always taught him to be proud, face up to everything and everybody and not to bow to another man. Now he asked him to do the opposite.

"You have always taught me to be strong but now you are telling me to be humble. Shouldn't I be proud?"

A satisfied smile flashed over his father's face and Kito knew that the explanation was clever.

"Kito you can be proud and humble at the same time. You can be proud of being a man with unlimited potential but you have to be humble because that potential is a gift to you."

"How do I teach this to my child? This is so difficult to understand."

"A child learns by copying adults. You teach a child to be humble by being humble yourself."

"How do I be humble?"

"It is difficult to generalize, because there are an unlimited number of situations in our lives. In each one we can behave in an arrogant or humble manner. Modesty is a state of mind which guides your actions, but I'll tell you an experience in my life which might clarify for you the concept of modesty - not that I was humble then.

"Remember I told you I had to leave the bay and return to Johannesburg because I had a contract to do an ad campaign. When you do an ad you must always think about your target audience and which of their weaknesses can be exploited. The idea is to sell. I looked for the benefit of the electric toothbrush, which I would promote, and I saw there were no positive aspects to this contraption. This made me realize that I was misleading people into buying something they didn't need. On the contrary, there were serious negative aspects which I called the electric toothbrush syndrome."

"That is a fancy name. What is this syndrome?"

"Yes, the name might be fancy, but the consequences were serious. I grasped that what I did was totally counter-productive. I had worked to create a need for something that was not only useless, but negative. Other people were employed making something else, which might be equally pointless, in order to buy something that is useless. All people employed in producing these products were wasting time, energy and natural resources.

"The negative effects of this activity were that all the mines, dams and roads that were built to supply raw materials and energy polluted the environment, took space away from other species and drove them to extinction."

"So how did you do the campaign if you couldn't find any positive aspect of the electric toothbrush?"

"I aimed the advert at man's vanity and envy. A man who has no confidence in his own ability tries to impress others with what is regarded as valuable - material possessions. When one man obtains something the other feels less worthy if he doesn't have it too, especially if it is fashionable. He works harder and longer, to try to prove his worth and you have a customer."

"Was the campaign a success?"

"Yes, it was. The market share of the company which produced this toothbrush increased, as did the general trend of sales. That was the last advert I ever made.

"You see, one example of humbleness would be not to buy an electric toothbrush or similar useless products, and to teach your child about the negative affects of the electric toothbrush syndrome. This would effect positively many aspects of your and your child's life." His father concluded.

"If I was humble and everybody else was humble what kind of a world would we create?" asked Kito trying to envision the world his father was asking him to help create.

"Well, you are not very humble in the number of questions you are asking," laughed Rurik. "I am tired. Let's go to sleep now and I'll try to answer your questions tomorrow when my brain is rested and is operating at its peak."

Kito's father stretched onto the pile of grass and closed his eyes. Kito lay on the hard ground and thought how nice it would be to sleep in a bed. His own fatigue soon overtook his now diffused thoughts, and he slipped into a world of dreams.

It was still cool when they pushed off in the morning. Kito was half asleep as he sat in the front of the mokoro while Rurik poled. They drove in silence and Kito listened to the rhythmical noise of the pole entering the water and the reeds scraping the sides of the mokoro. When Kito opened his eyes his father smiled.

"I am glad you decided to wake up, my boy. I thought you had been bitten by the tsetse fly and got sleeping sickness. I am so happy I was wrong. Now you can take my place and get some exercise."

"I didn't think you were very alert when we started this morning. You drove into the papyrus a few times," teased Kito.

"I was just trying to wake you up, but I must admit not very successfully, so I gave up." His father chuckled

"You keep telling me not to give up, then you give me a bad example. Let me pole before you give up on that too," Kito said and took the pole from his father.

His father walked to the front and sat down, taking some dried snake meat and chewing reluctantly. He then leaned against the front of the mokoro and looked at Kito.

"I think I owe you an answer to your question of last night. Now that you have woken up I am ready to discharge my obligation to your question on the effects of humbleness on society."

Kito could see his father was in high spirits this morning; it made him feel confident.

"Okay Dad. That wasn't exactly the question I asked, but we have nothing else to do so I will listen."

With a mock frown on his face his father said: "I will answer your question, but before I do I think I should impress on you a value that will stand you in good stead."

"And what is that?"

"To be humble to a mind superior to yours." His father burst out laughing.

"Why, and whose is it?" Kito asked with a mischievous grin.

It isn't necessary to answer the second part of your question. That part is obvious. You have to be humble because it would take the cockiness out of you and you will be back to normal. Humbleness will make you learn. You will know how much you don't know and you will not know enough."

"One thing I know for sure is that you don't enjoy snake meat. Your expression is very humble when you swallow." Kito laughed heartily.

"Well my son, you will know even better how humbling it is when you eat snake meat because that is the only food we have. This is a practical example that humbleness aids conservation. Humbleness modifies our perceptions of material and spiritual wealth. Materiality gives way to spirituality. Such a change in thinking has a dramatic effect and the individual and the world becomes richer and happier."

Kito saw his dad was serious now and concentrated hard on what he was saying. "How can we be richer and happier with less material wealth?" he asked.

"Prosperity is not how much you have, but how little you need to be satisfied. The biggest problem of modern society is the stress that comes from the need to acquire, or maintain the level of material wealth. If we accepted that we don't need all the things we are striving for, our stress would reduce, and we would have more time to do the things we really want to do."

This made sense to Kito and he wondered why people worked so hard for things, instead of having fun. He recognized how complicated and irrational society is. Their life in the bay had been happy and they used very little, but still had lots of fun.

"What do you think man should do?" Kito asked.

"He could study subjects which interested him and educate himself in a new line of work, like conservation. Mankind could have as its aim, making the earth a Garden of Eden. We could reforest the Earth. Resources should be directed at research and practical application of solar energy. That would reduce pollution and the demand for natural resources and space used in power generation. Man would be paid for rebuilding and not destroying. If we pay man to produce something we don't need, which is at the same time destructive to the environment and our quality of life, we should gladly pay him for doing something that would improve our environment and quality of life.

"Quality should be rewarded and quality takes time and thought. Some furniture has lasted for centuries. It was looked after because it was beautiful and today it still has great value. Only one tree was cut to make a chair or table instead of many. Nobody in his right mind would throw away furniture made for Louis XIV, or a Stradivarius violin. The mind of Leonardo da Vinci still lives in the painting of the Mona Lisa and enriches us. It took Leonardo seven years to create this masterpiece. Today we replace cars and furniture every few years. A few splashes of paint on canvas, or the imprints of a chicken running across it, we call art but it really is a waste of canvas and paint.

"If every person in the world saves one match a day we would save more than five billion matches. If each of those matches weighs a gram it would represent a saving of five thousand tons a day, or two million trees weighing a ton each, every year. A forest. If we continue to plunder Earth she will fight back and we will lose."

Kito stared with wide open eyes at his father. He had never seen him talking so passionately, but what amazed him most was the logic of his words and the vast possibilities for improvement.

"How will nature fight back?" he asked.

"Nature is already fighting back and we are losing. We have the ozone hole and a greenhouse effect. There is an increase in skin cancer and stress-related diseases. Tuberculosis and other diseases that we thought were eradicated, are coming back and are not responding to the antibiotics.

"We cannot win the fight against nature. We are incidental in this struggle and if we are not careful we could become extinct too."

"This is frightening! How do we avoid this?" Kito asked concerned.

"Kito don't be frightened. I am telling you what could happen if we don't change, but if we grew spiritually we would value human spirit more than material wealth and reduce pressure on the environment.

"There are people who value human spirit, but their efforts are not recognized, because they are not directly involved in creating material wealth. Teachers are the best examples. Throughout the world teacher's rewards are mediocre and because of that we attract very few of the best brains to the profession. Because they don't produce things but *only* impart knowledge, their contribution to society isn't highly rated. We should elevate teachers to the pinnacle of society and honor them more than any other profession. Then society would prosper.

"If we attract mediocrity to channel young minds, mediocrity is what we are going to get and society will deteriorate further. Each child in the world should be schooled and given proper education. There is the argument that funds are not available, but it is a case of misdirection of resources on the part of governments.

"Thousands of billions are spent on weapons of mass destruction which don't enhance but endanger our security. If that money was spent on education, every child in the world could be educated. In an educated world we wouldn't need weapons.

"People should demand total disarmament from their governments. Governments ought to work according to the wishes of the people. They don't. But could be compelled to, if people took their destiny into their own hands, instead of leaving it in the hands of inefficient and misdirected bureaucracies."

"Has there always been government?" asked Kito.

"Yes. And we do need government to co-ordinate our efforts but not bureaucracies which rule our lives. Our governments should be made up of teachers. Not rulers. We should be free men and not revenue providing slaves.

"We could be free if we realize that responsibility comes with freedom. There would be no need for huge apparatus to regulate our behaviour. Our responsibility is to respect other men and other species and then we would have the freedom we had given others. How to achieve these aims is what our governments should be teaching us, but then they would not have much control over our lives and would be forced to do something productive, which is much harder than spending our money and telling us what to do."

"What can we do to change this?" asked Kito. He was learning about a crazy world he hadn't even known existed. Only now he saw how lucky he was to have had parents that had isolated him from this madness.

"One could formulate some kind of dramatic message and find a way to reach like-thinking individuals. They would in turn spread the message further until the movement becomes so strong that politicians will be compelled to take notice."

"What would your message be?"

"The message would have to be basic, to the point, and give hope for a better future."

"So what would it be?" Kito asked impatiently.

A frown furrowed his father's forehead and his eyes narrowed. Kito knew his father was concentrating to find an answer and wasn't so sure what the message should be. Then he started talking in a booming voice.

"To all free-thinking individuals of the world.

"You have heard all about the world being doomed, but there *is* a future for us and our children, if we act now. We must use our unlimited mental abilities to change the course along which we are being guided by artificial values. Let's leave a better world for our children than the one we have inherited. Irrespective of color, creed or gender we are the children of one father and our destiny is common. Let's join our minds together and we can do it. Only the belief that we cannot will prevent us from succeeding. If we fail to act, *then* the world is doomed.

"Let's enter the age of idealism where despair won't have a place.

All structures built by man can be changed and improved. Let's do it.

"Only lunatics need apply."

Kito applauded. "That is a powerful message, but why the last sentence?"

"The last sentence is for the critics. That sentence is going to tell them that they are predictable. It will also have an attraction value, because it is out of character with the rest of the message. People will wonder why it is there and study the meaning of the message more carefully. Individuals who believe in the power of their minds will be receptive to the idea. Each of them could then improve the message, or create another, better one, to suit their perception and area of interest."

"What would they do then?" Kito was getting excited.

"They would spread the message and start freeing the minds with which they communicate from fear and oppression caused by either criminals or governments."

"Sounds like you don't think that there is much difference."

"They have their similarities. Both take by force or stealth, and spend clandestinely." Kito's father snickered.

"How would you advertise? Doesn't it cost money?" Kito was learning how important money was in this world.

"Yes, initially it would cost some money, but if the first advertisement drew a response there would be people working voluntarily, pooling their financial and mental resources. Don't forget that there would be a great concentration of mind power between the individuals that appreciate the potential of the message. They would target the sections of the population they knew best, so funds would be spent effectively. You must remember something else. Money is only a commodity and a very unstable one. Sometimes it is worth a lot and sometimes not. Depending on how wasteful the government is. There is a commodity which is much more valuable than money and which always has great value. It is the mind of man. It created money. If you mobilize minds you have all the power you need. I would go for mind, instead of for money, anytime. If you succeed in reaching Hollywood it would be a great achievement. Hollywood, at the moment, has the biggest influence on mass morality. Many people there are questioning the values by which they have lived, so there is a good chance of success."

"Do you think this could succeed?" Kito asked anxiously.

"Yes, I think there is a fair chance. There would be many arguments against this proposal. The first would be that this is a dream and too idealistic to work, but I think, if we don't have a dream we don't have a future. Dreamers have given the world some of the greatest insights."

All this made sense to Kito. He couldn't understand what made man work against his own good. Maybe his father could explain that to him, too.

"Why didn't your generation do something to change the way it lived?" he asked.

"It is difficult to change the values by which one lives. It is so ingrained in our makeup that it takes great effort to change one's habits. People were so busy trying to comply with expectations created by society that they had neither time nor energy to concentrate on change. Any change requires much greater effort than going along established paths. You can compare it with a rolling stone. To keep the stone rolling, once it is going, requires very little energy. If it is rolling downhill it takes effort to stop it and even more effort to start rolling it back uphill.

"I think my generation is just starting to understand that the stone needs to be stopped and effort has to be put into it. Otherwise it will roll out of control and then we won't be able to stop it anymore. I think uncertainty about the future is making people question the values by which they live. The world is confused. There is one good thing about confusion. Clarity always follows, sometimes though, too late. We didn't do enough because we believed that the system in which we lived was the best we could do. Our minds were controlled by the propaganda of politicians. These people are skilled in manipulation and work on man's greed. They create tensions because in times of tension they are more important and are in the public eye. They appear to be resolving the world's problems. While resolving these problems they have created, they fly first class, live in the best hotels and wine and dine each other, with our money. They smile in public and laugh in private. If they do not agree, they send suckers like us to kill and die for the mess they have created. If there is a peaceful solution to the problem, in many cases it has nothing to do with justice, but everything to do with the well-being of the politician involved. Only now I fully understand how important it is to voice my opposition to this state of affairs, to demand change in the wasteful structures of governments, so you can have a better future, my son.

"Throughout the world corporations are downsizing to eliminate bureaucracy and improve productivity. It is about time for governments to do the same. Governments must become what they are so generously paid for, civil servants, but in much reduced numbers. We don't need so many servants to tell us what to do." Rurik's voice was forceful and his eyes hard.

"Dad, you sound like you are going to do something about it."

"Yes, I will. I promise you, from now on I will fight, more than I ever did before, for your and your children's future and for all the inhabitants of this world whose rights are being denied."

Silence enveloped the mokoro. Kito wasn't alarmed about his future anymore. His father always did what he said he was going to do. Kito didn't know how, but he believed his father would change things. He admired him so much for his strength.

"What are you going to do?" he asked.

"I will tell people about a world infinitely better than the one in which we live, and help them order their thoughts. Then we will start a campaign for change."

"What makes you think you will succeed where nobody has succeeded before?" Kito enquired.

"For thousands of years man lived without the wheel. Then he discovered the wheel."

"So you will discover the wheel?"

"Maybe not, but I can help. There are other people working for a better world. I could help them."

"And you think you could succeed?" Kito wanted to be a member of this team.

"Why not? A determined man with an open mind has unlimited potential. The world is ready for change. The majority is unhappy with the present situation and would support change. All we need is wise leadership."

"Who would lead us?"

"Jesus."

Kito couldn't believe it. Had his father gone mad? Up until now he had spoken sensibly.

"But Jesus is not alive!" he said.

"Yes He is. He is alive in His teachings and His thoughts are with us. If we study them, try to understand them and follow them we would have leadership unrivalled in its wisdom. We would have an all-encompassing philosophy which would lead us along a straight path."

"Is Jesus a God or man?"

"I don't know. All I know is that I subscribe to his philosophy now more than ever, except for turning the other cheek."

"So we could become disciples of Jesus?" asked Kito incredulously.

"Yes, we could and we should."

To Kito this was a fascinating discovery. As the days passed he asked questions about the philosophies Jesus had taught and slowly a perfect society took shape in his mind. It was natural and logical. He envisaged a life on earth of peaceful co-existence between people and between man and other species.

Through their discussions, his and his father's minds were freed and their imaginations ran wild. They spoke about the potential of a free man and a perfect society he could create. They imagined a world in which animals roamed Africa and the world, unrestricted and free in restored forests. They longed for this world of peace and understanding. They dreamed and dreamed.

* * * *

In the morning of the tenth day on the mokoro, Kito spotted a sign of man. A column of smoke was rising straight into the air above the distant forest. It was a big cloud of smoke produced by a fire like they would have made, before Madala taught them that it was much easier to have a small fire.

"There is smoke!" Kito shouted, pointing excitedly.

His father jumped up, a Coca-Cola can with which he was bailing water in his hand. With an incredulous expression he stared at the distant smoke. When he turned to Kito happiness radiated from his eyes.

"Kito, we have done it! Against all odds," he said and smiled widely. Eyes shining, he firmly hugged Kito.

"My son, I have always known you were a brave boy but through the ordeal we have experienced I realized how wrong I was. You are not a boy. You are a man and I am very proud to be your father. But there is one other thing I want you to know. If I was the man on the chimney I would never have let you go." His father's voice choked.

"I know Dad. I have always known that." Kito said, tears welling in his eyes.

He thought he saw moisture in his father's eyes, but his father quickly turned and walked to the front of the mokoro and stood looking at the smoke. For the first time, now that they were going to meet people, Kito realized that the clothes they had been wearing for almost two months were in tatters.

His father's trouser legs were cut off. His shirt torn and without buttons was held by his belt on which a knife, axe and survival kit hung. Kito didn't look much better either. He felt uncomfortable at the thought that they would meet people looking like this.

His father stood proud and strong, despite his rags.

Now that they were about to achieve their objective of getting back to civilization, Kito's emotions were mixed. This meant the end of an adventure and the comradeship which had developed between him and his father, as equal members of a team. The understanding of each other that they had developed was immeasurably more than they had had before the swamp. Kito understood how much he loved his father and how much his father loved him. That knowledge reinstated the security he hadn't had when their plane took off from Johannesburg. He hoped they wouldn't go back there. He was sad at the thought of leaving this world which he had entered unsettled and confused and which he was leaving emotionally and spiritually enriched.

"I feel sad," Kito said.

"My son, every achievement has its disappointments. When we achieve our aim we realize that that is not after all everything we desire, and we are confused until we set a new aim for ourselves. No achievement can give you absolute happiness, otherwise you would stagnate. But there is always a new mountain to climb."

The shots, coming from the direction of the smoke sounded very unnatural and shattered the peacefulness of the swamp. His father hurriedly turned forward and cocked his head to listen. Everything was quiet again.

"Dad, who could that be shooting?"

"These must be licensed hunters. If they were poachers they wouldn't be making a fire." His father's voice was hard and brittle with anger, his hands clenched into fists and he stood unmoving until they broke through the last reeds and encountered civilization.

They saw three four-wheel drive vehicles with logos on the sides, all new and painted green. The men and women were fashionably dressed. The men held rifles in their hands and gesticulated excitedly. They were grouped around something that was hidden by one of the vehicles.

Kito and his father walked closer and saw what all the excitement was about. A dead elephant was lying on the ground and a group of natives were hacking off the tusks so the hunters would have a trophy to put above the fireplace.

Kito looked at his father and saw his lips tightly pressed together, a grimace of fury on his face and a frightening rage in his eyes.

They were almost upon the nearest vehicle when the hacking stopped and the crowd began to break-up. A woman saw them first. She looked at them and started laughing. The others followed the direction of her pointed finger and joined in the mocking laughter.

The ridicule hurt Kito's pride. He couldn't make himself look at his father. He hung his head in shame, unable to comprehend the morality of people who ridiculed others for their appearance and laughed with pleasure, while the elephant they had just killed lay at their feet.

He looked at them, wanting to shout how wrong they were, when he saw two natives lift one of the tusks on their shoulders to carry it to the fourwheel drive. It was curved at the bottom, a gash in the shape of a bow clearly visible.

With anguish he looked at his father and saw the shock on his face.

"They have killed Emperor."

"Yes my son. They have killed him."

His father's face darkened by the shadow of sadness was foreboding and ominous.

"Why did they do it? He did them no harm," Kito said trying to hold back the tears.

"No my son, he did them no harm. Man kills for pleasure and vanity. I am sure they have a licence from the government, which cost them a few thousand dollars. I am ashamed to belong to the race of man." His voice was hard and the outrage in his eyes frightened Kito.

Kito felt hot tears of grief scald his eyes and in a flood they broke through, watering the fertile soil of Africa with more bitterness, as he searched for words that would ease his father's pain.

"Dad, I see the mountains clearly now," he said and hugged his father. "I will fight injustice."

His father gripped him firmly and his resolute voice drowned the mocking laughter.

"We will fight, my son. *Together*."

The End